The Sand Seas of Mars: Repairing the Rover

by Jason M. Burns

illustrated by Dustin Evans

TGP TORCH GRAPHIC PRESS

Published in the United States of America by Cherry Lake Publishing Group
Ann Arbor, Michigan
www.cherrylakepublishing.com

Reading Adviser: Beth Walker Gambro, MS, Ed., Reading Consultant, Yorkville, IL

Book Designer: Book Buddy Media

Torch Graphic Press is an imprint of Cherry Lake Publishing Group.

Library of Congress Cataloging-in-Publication Data has been filed and is available at catalog.loc.gov

Cherry Lake Publishing Group would like to acknowledge the work of the Partnership for 21st Century Learning, a Network of Battelle for Kids. Please visit http://www.battelleforkids.org/networks/p21 for more information.

Printed in the United States of America
Corporate Graphics

TABLE OF CONTENTS

Mission log: July 22, 2055.

Dad and I have arrived on Mars with my friend, Daniela. Astronaut training prepared us for the trip, but not for the sights. It is so amazing here! We will be visiting the sand seas of Mars today. I can't wait to draw the kinds of **Martians** that might live there. Daniela has promised to help me with the science. This is going to be the best summer vacation ever.

—Malcolm Thomas

artians: living creatures of Mars

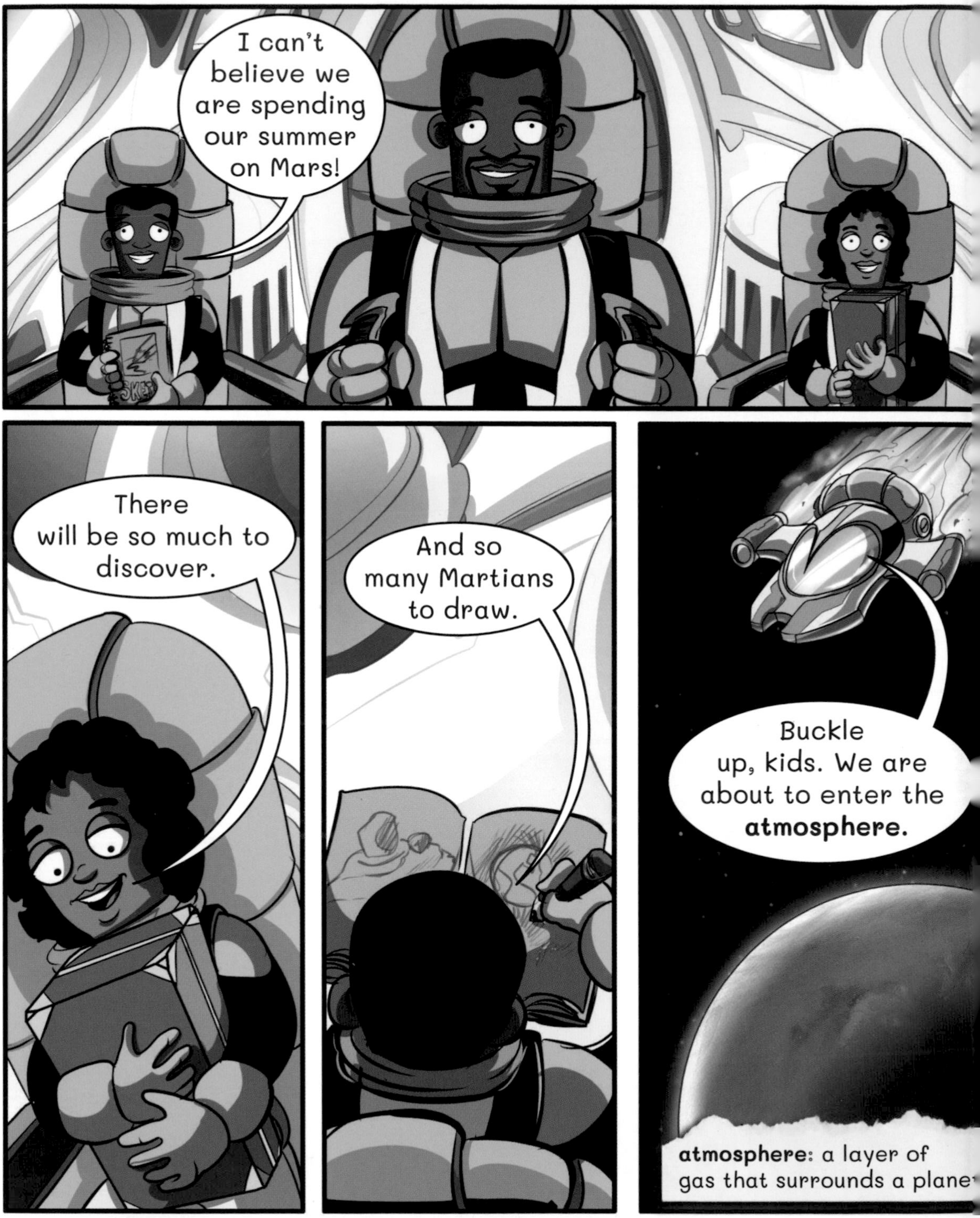
I can't believe we are spending our summer on Mars!
There will be so much to discover.
And so many Martians to draw.
Buckle up, kids. We are about to enter the **atmosphere.**

atmosphere: a layer of gas that surrounds a plane

MARS FACT

The atmosphere of Mars is 95 percent carbon dioxid
That is much different than the atmosphere of Earth,
which is mostly nitrogen and oxygen.

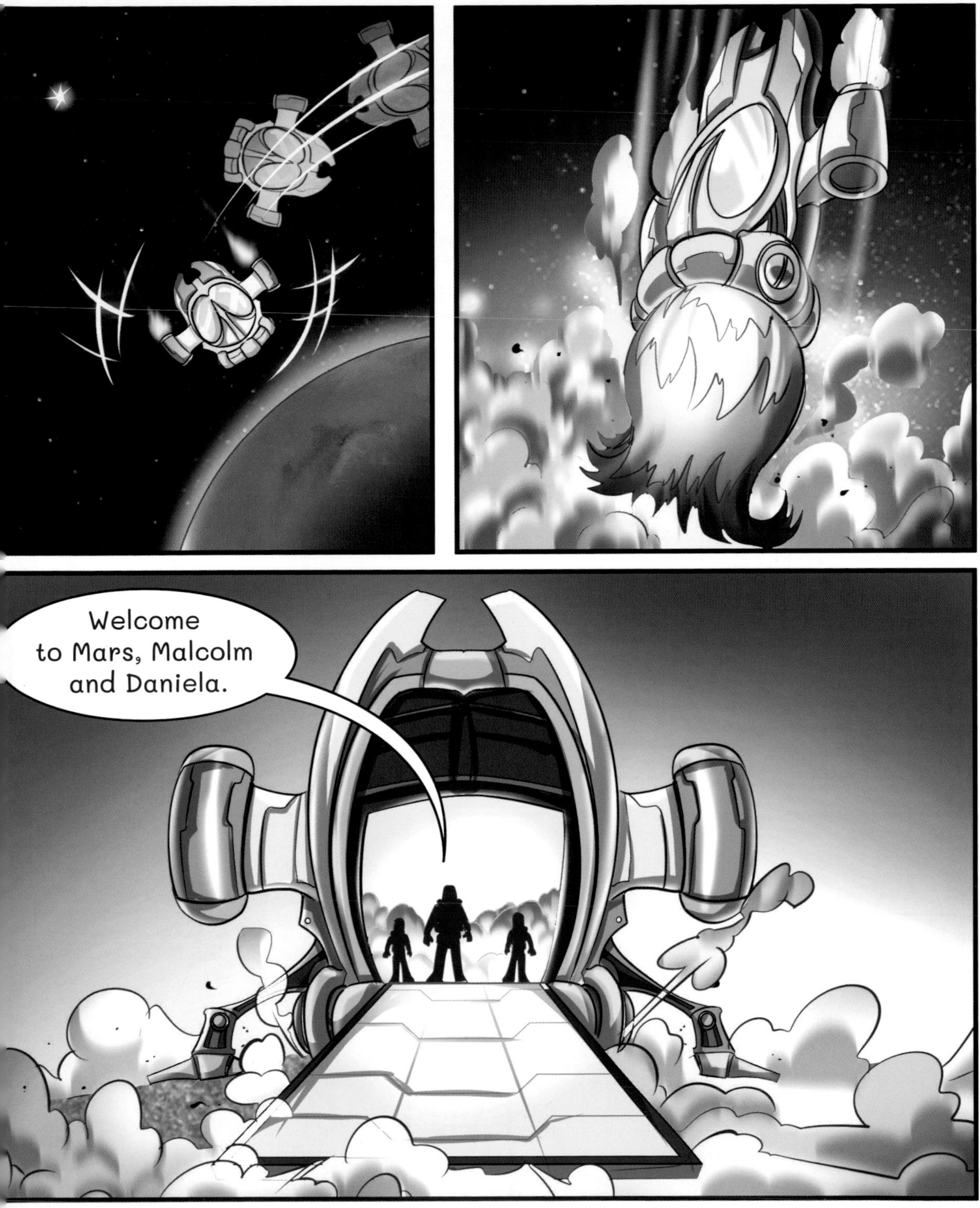
Welcome to Mars, Malcolm and Daniela.

MARS FACT

In 1610, Galileo Galilei was the first person to look at Mars through a telescope. Before, astronomers had observed the planet and noticed it was brighter at different times. Galileo was the first to use a telescope to record Mars's orbit.

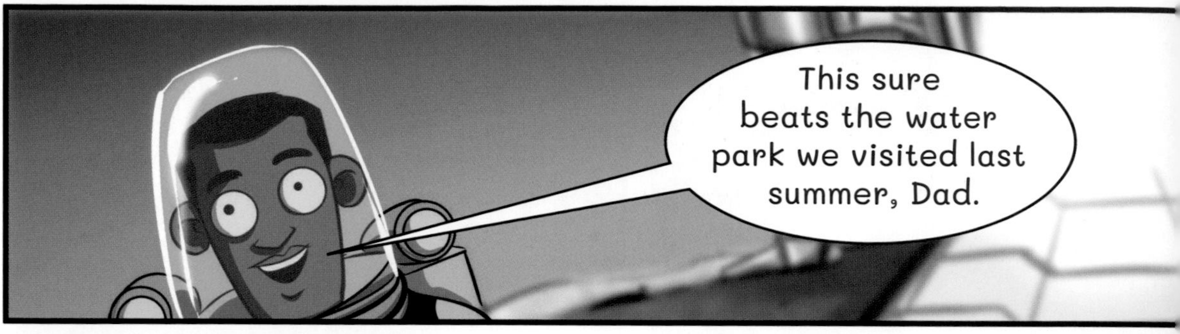
This sure beats the water park we visited last summer, Dad.

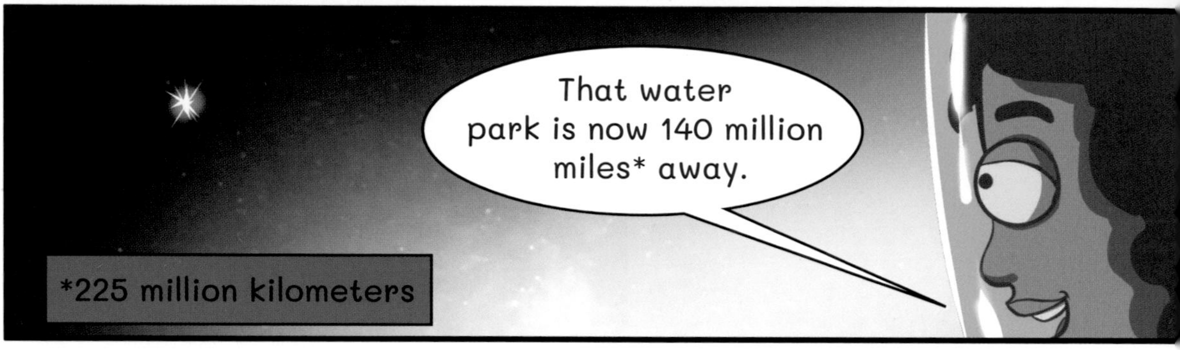
That water park is now 140 million miles* away.
*225 million kilometers

MARS FACT

It takes 6 to 8 months to travel to Mars from Earth. In comparison, it takes only 3 days to reach the Moon by space shuttle.

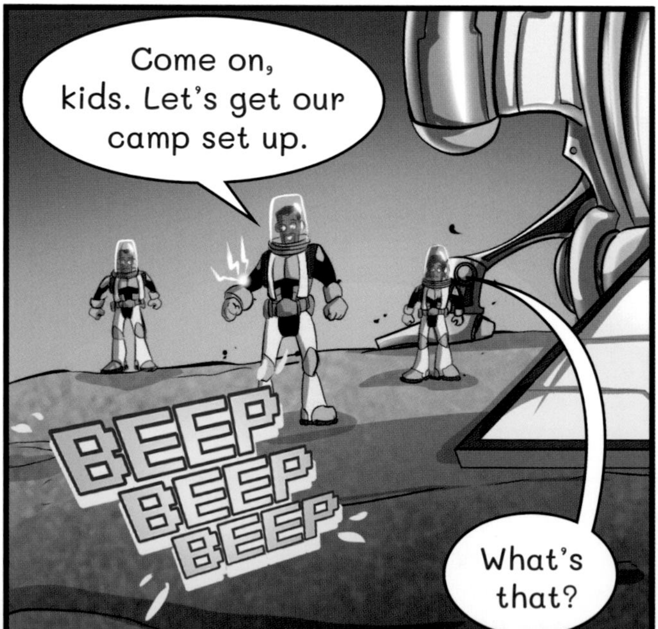
Come on, kids. Let's get our camp set up.
BEEP BEEP BEEP
What's that?

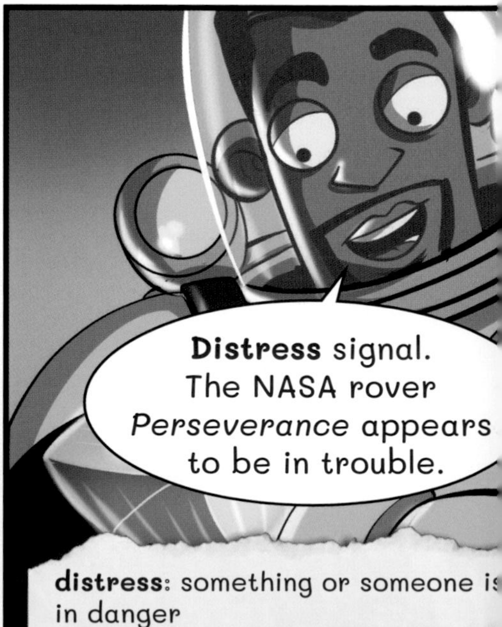
Distress signal. The NASA rover *Perseverance* appears to be in trouble.
distress: something or someone is in danger

THE CASE FOR SPACE

People thought Mars was a bright star for centuries. Thanks to modern-day science, we now know a lot more about it!

•Mars was named for the Roman god of war.

•The Greeks called it Ares, after their own war god.

•The planet's red color reminded the Greeks of bloody war battles.

•Mars also has 2 small moons with ties to ancient folklore. They are Phobos and Deimos.

•Phobos and Deimos were discovered by Asaph Hall in 1877.

•The moons were named after the horses that pulled Ares's war chariot. In English their names mean fear (Phobos) and panic (Deimos).

•Both moons look like asteroids. They may actually be asteroids that were caught in Mars's gravity.

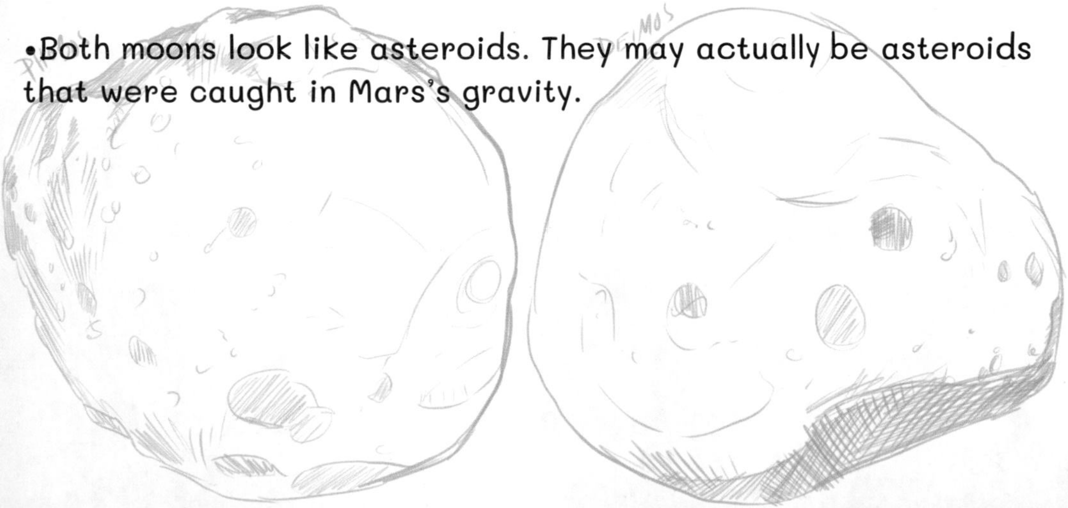

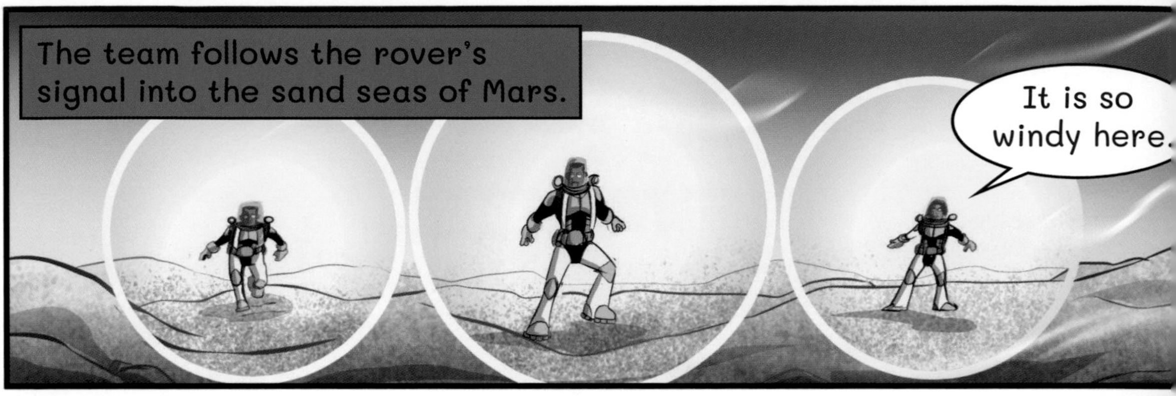
The team follows the rover's signal into the sand seas of Mars.
It is so windy here.

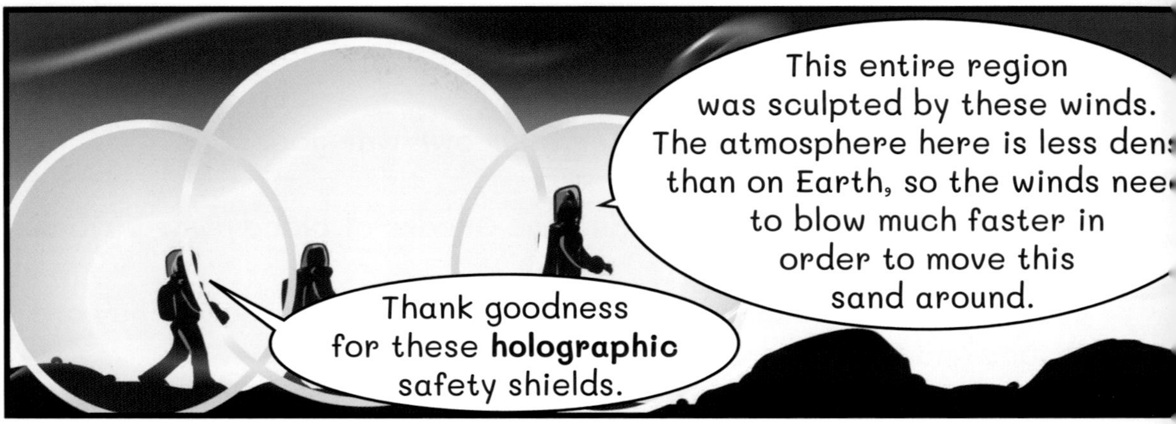
This entire region was sculpted by these winds. The atmosphere here is less den
than on Earth, so the winds nee
to blow much faster in order to move this sand around.
Thank goodness for these **holographic** safety shields.

MARS FACT

In the northern tip of Mars there is a sand sea that is one of the largest in the entire solar system. It is believed to be 6 times larger than the Mojave Desert in California.

holographic: created using laser lights; holograms are made by using lasers and bending the light with lenses

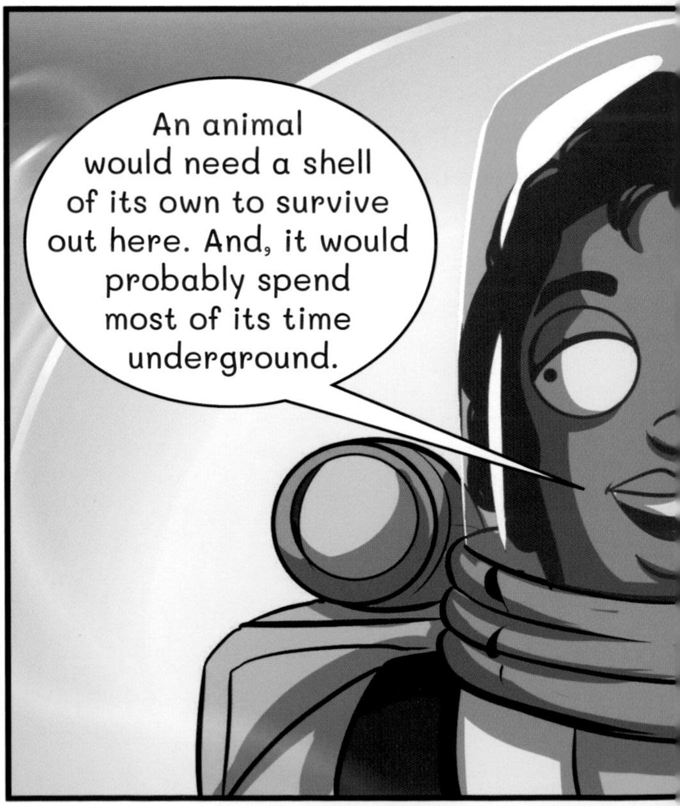
An animal would need a shell of its own to survive out here. And, it would probably spend most of its time underground.

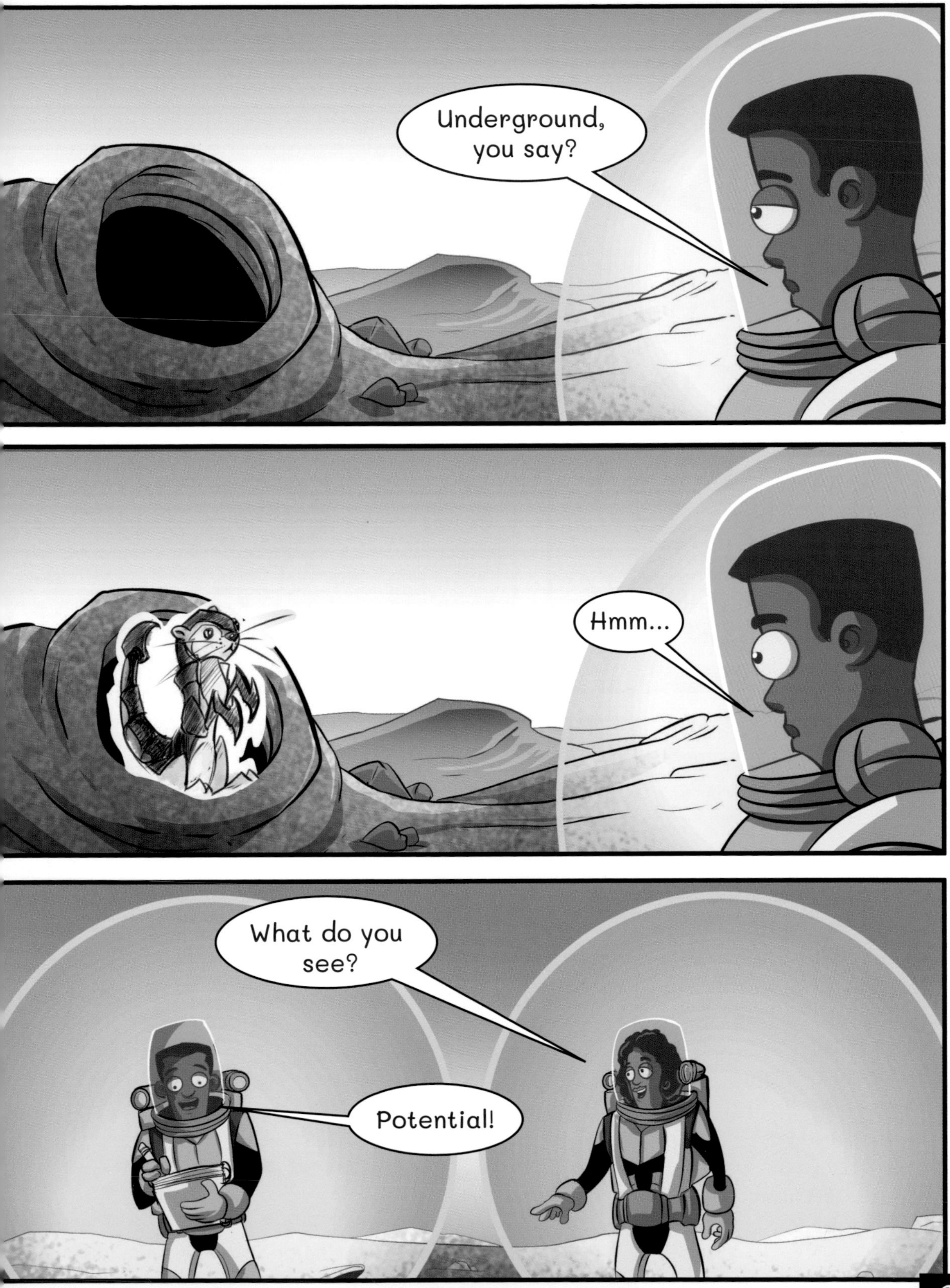

Underground, you say?
Hmm...
What do you see?
Potential!

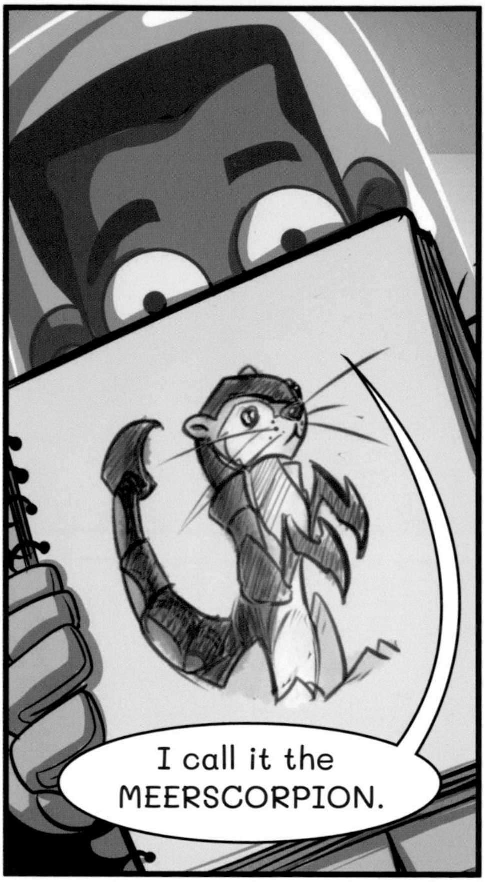
I call it the MEERSCORPION.

SCIENCE FACT

Native to Africa, meerkats live in underground burrows. These burrows hel the mammals escape the African heat an avoid predators.

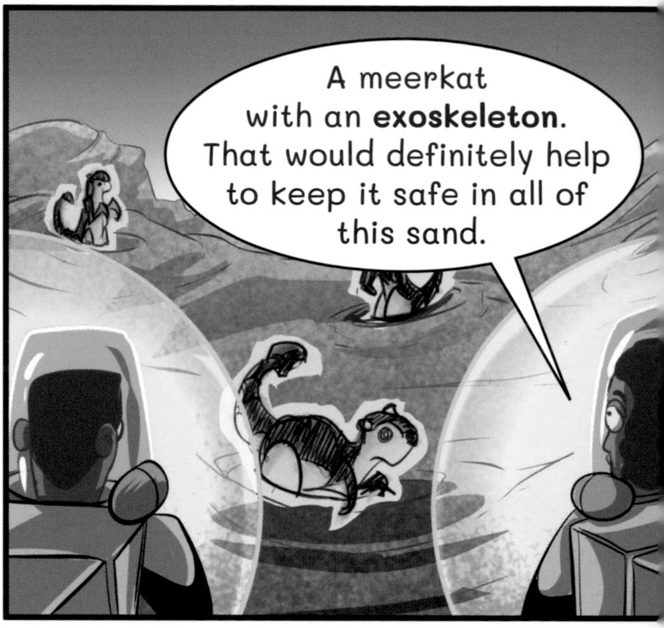
A meerkat with an **exoskeleton**. That would definitely help to keep it safe in all of this sand.

SCIENCE FACT

Many animals have exoskeletons on Earth, including crabs, beetles, and snails. Exoskeletons help protect and support the body of some animals, including invertebrates. Invertebrates are animals without backbones.

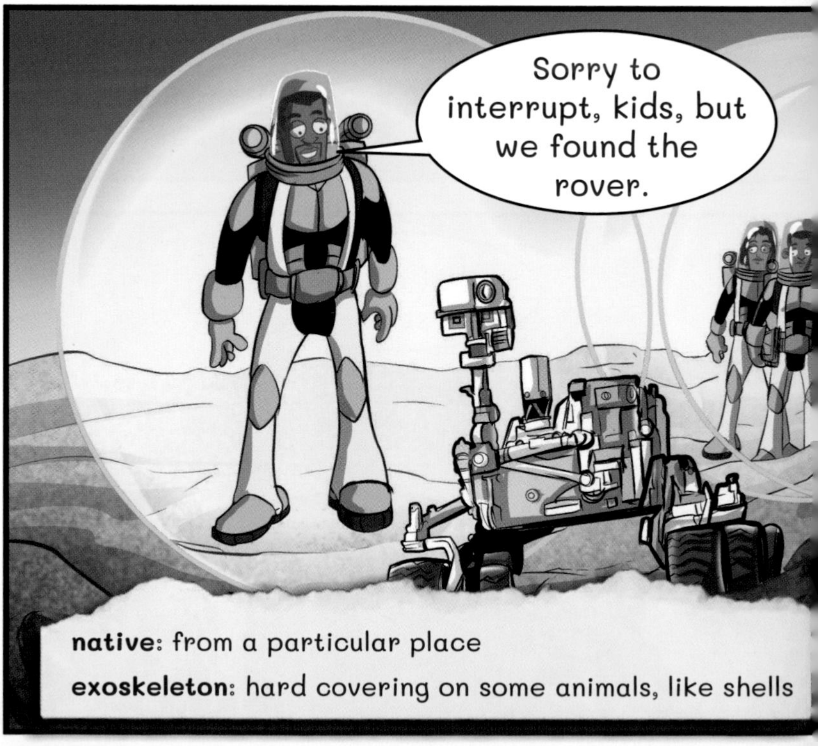
Sorry to interrupt, kids, but we found the rover.

native: from a particular place

exoskeleton: hard covering on some animals, like shells

THE SCIENCE OF SCIENCE FICTION

Finding a rover on Mars is more science than science fiction. There have been 5 robotic missions to Mars by NASA as of 2021. China also landed a rover in 2021. The NASA rovers have been named: *Sojourner*, *Spirit*, *Opportunity*, *Curiosity*, and *Perseverance*. Here are some facts about the most recent Mars rover, *Perseverance*.

•The mission of *Perseverance* is to search for evidence that life once existed on Mars.

•*Perseverance* will collect rock samples that will later be brought back to Earth.

•The mission launched on July 30, 2020. The rover landed on Mars on February 18, 2021.

•*Perseverance*'s mission is to spend 1 Mars year collecting samples on the planet. A single year on Mars is equal to 2 years on Earth. Because Mars is farther away from the Sun, it takes a longer amount of time for the planet to travel around it. An Earth year is 365 days. A Mars year is 687 days.

•*Perseverance* was equipped with new technology. This includes an **autonomous** navigation system. The system allows it to travel more quickly over the bumpy landscape.

•The Mars helicopter, *Ingenuity*, also hitched a ride onboard the rover. It made the first powered flight on another planet.

autonomous: can act on its own without being controlled

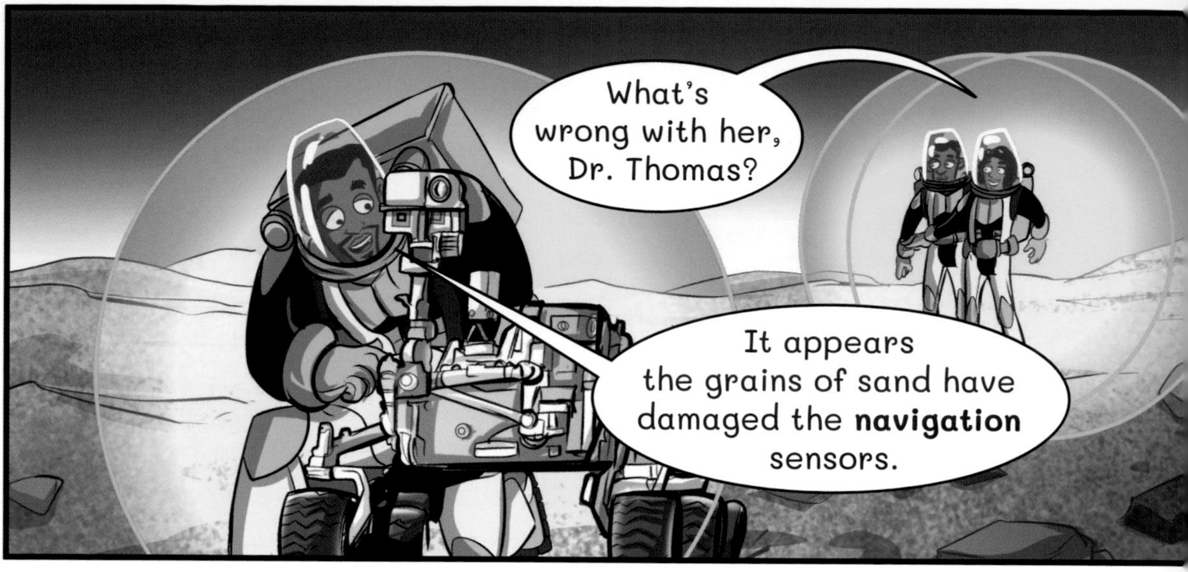
What's wrong with her, Dr. Thomas?
It appears the grains of sand have damaged the **navigation** sensors.

MARS FACT

Massive Mars sand storms have been witnessed by telescopes on Earth.

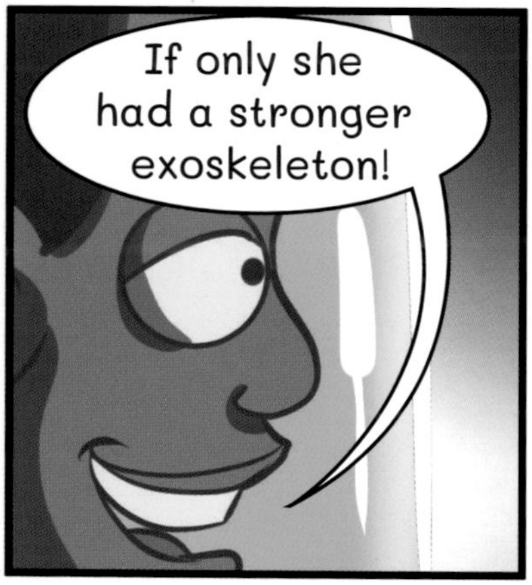
If only she had a stronger exoskeleton!

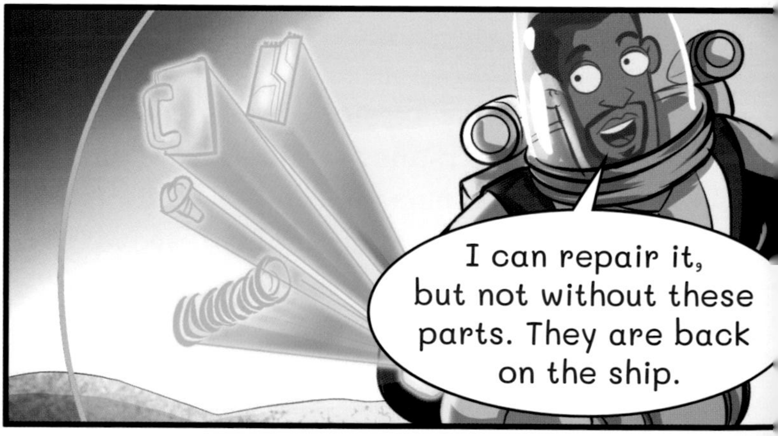
I can repair it, but not without these parts. They are back on the ship.

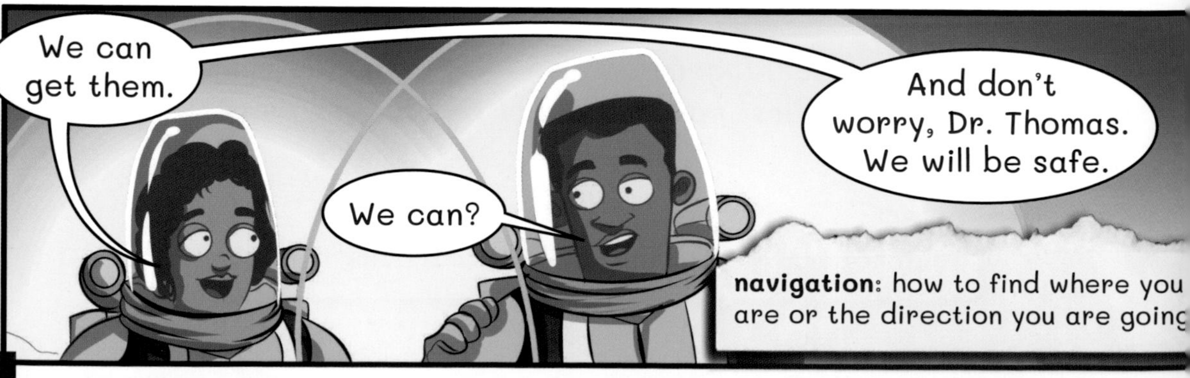
We can get them.
We can?
And don't worry, Dr. Thomas. We will be safe.
navigation: how to find where you are or the direction you are going

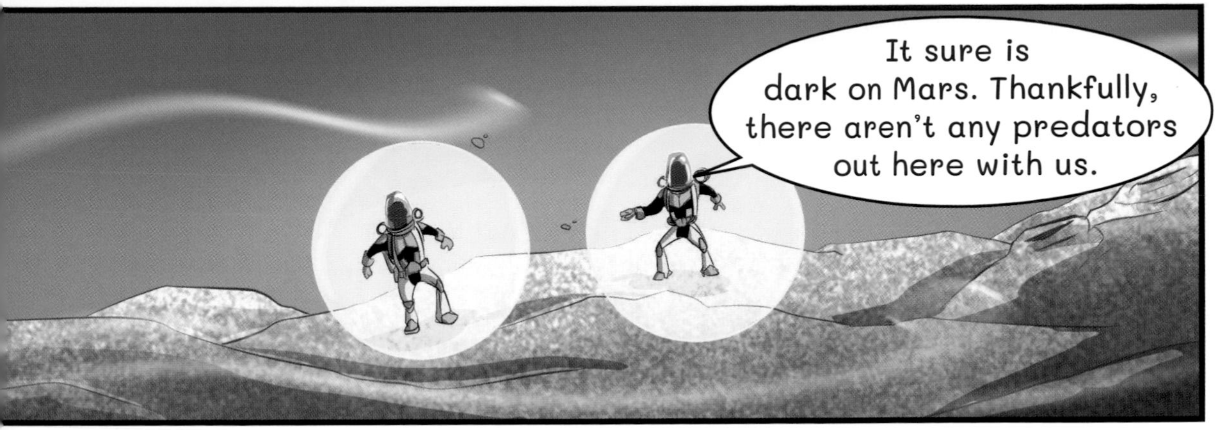
It sure is dark on Mars. Thankfully, there aren't any predators out here with us.

SCIENCE FACT

A predator is any animal that hunts and feeds on another animal for survival. On Earth, wolves, sharks, and lions are all examples of predators.

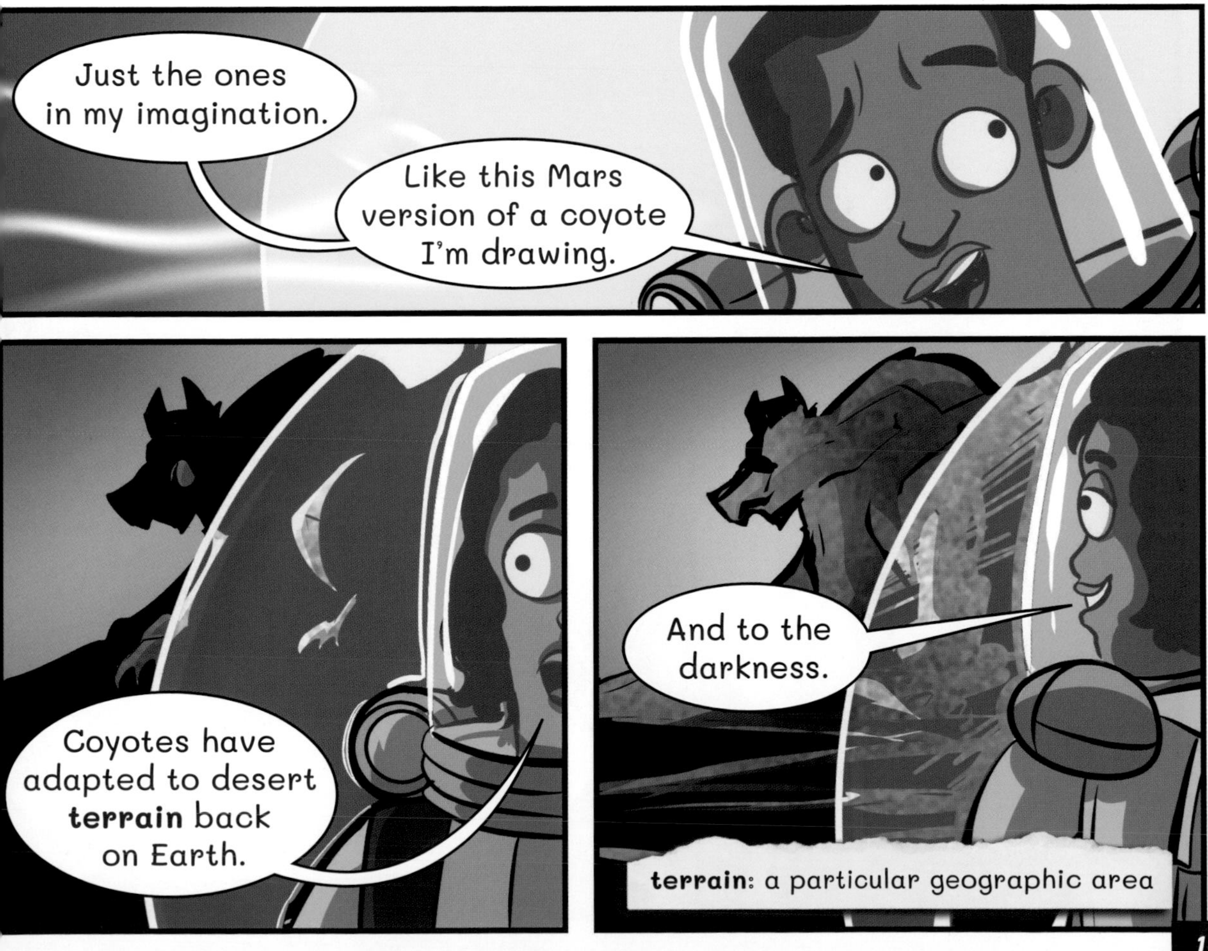
Just the ones in my imagination.
Like this Mars version of a coyote I'm drawing.
Coyotes have adapted to desert **terrain** back on Earth.
And to the darkness.

terrain: a particular geographic area

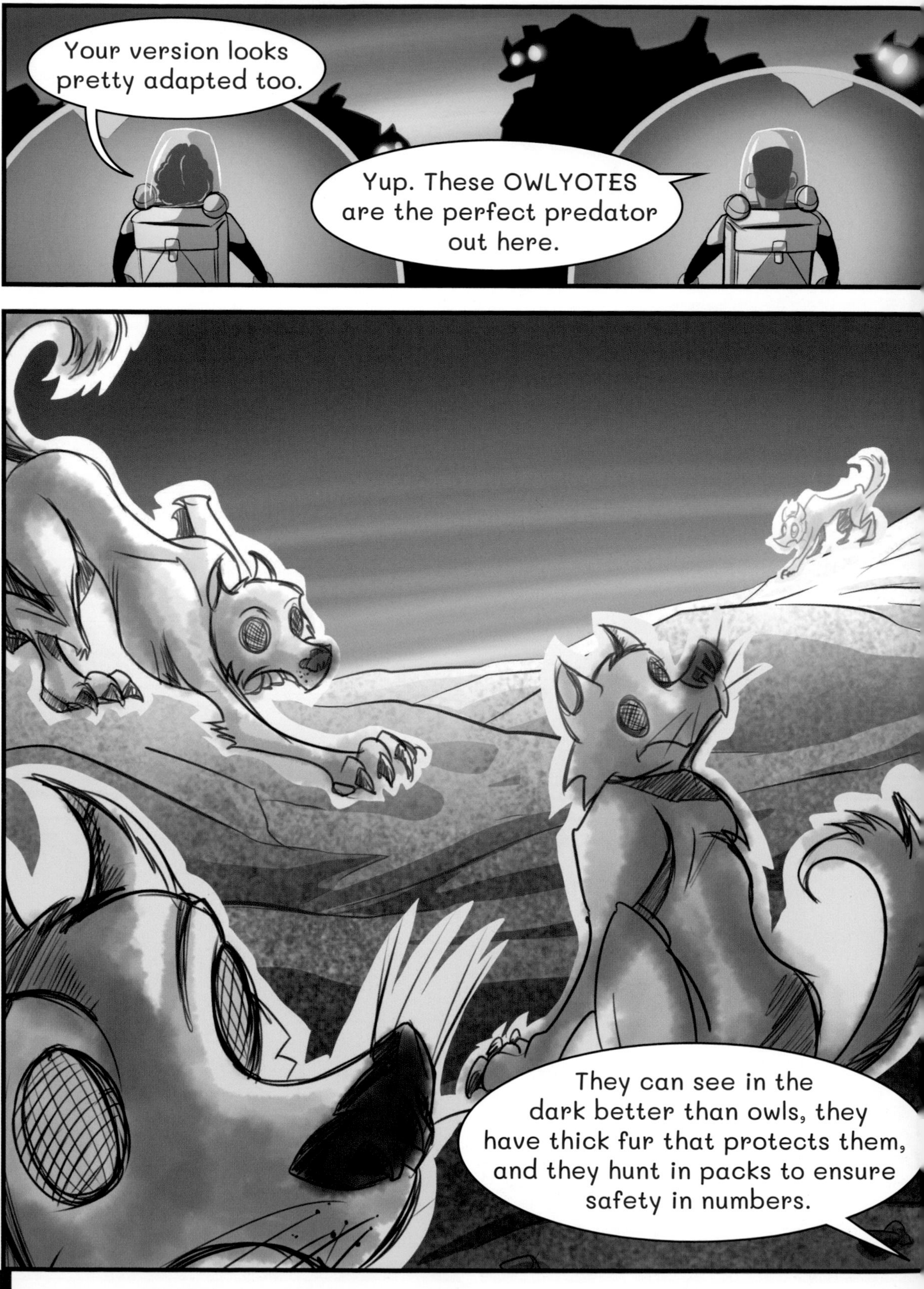

Your version looks pretty adapted too.
Yup. These OWLYOTES are the perfect predator out here.
They can see in the dark better than owls, they have thick fur that protects them, and they hunt in packs to ensure safety in numbers.

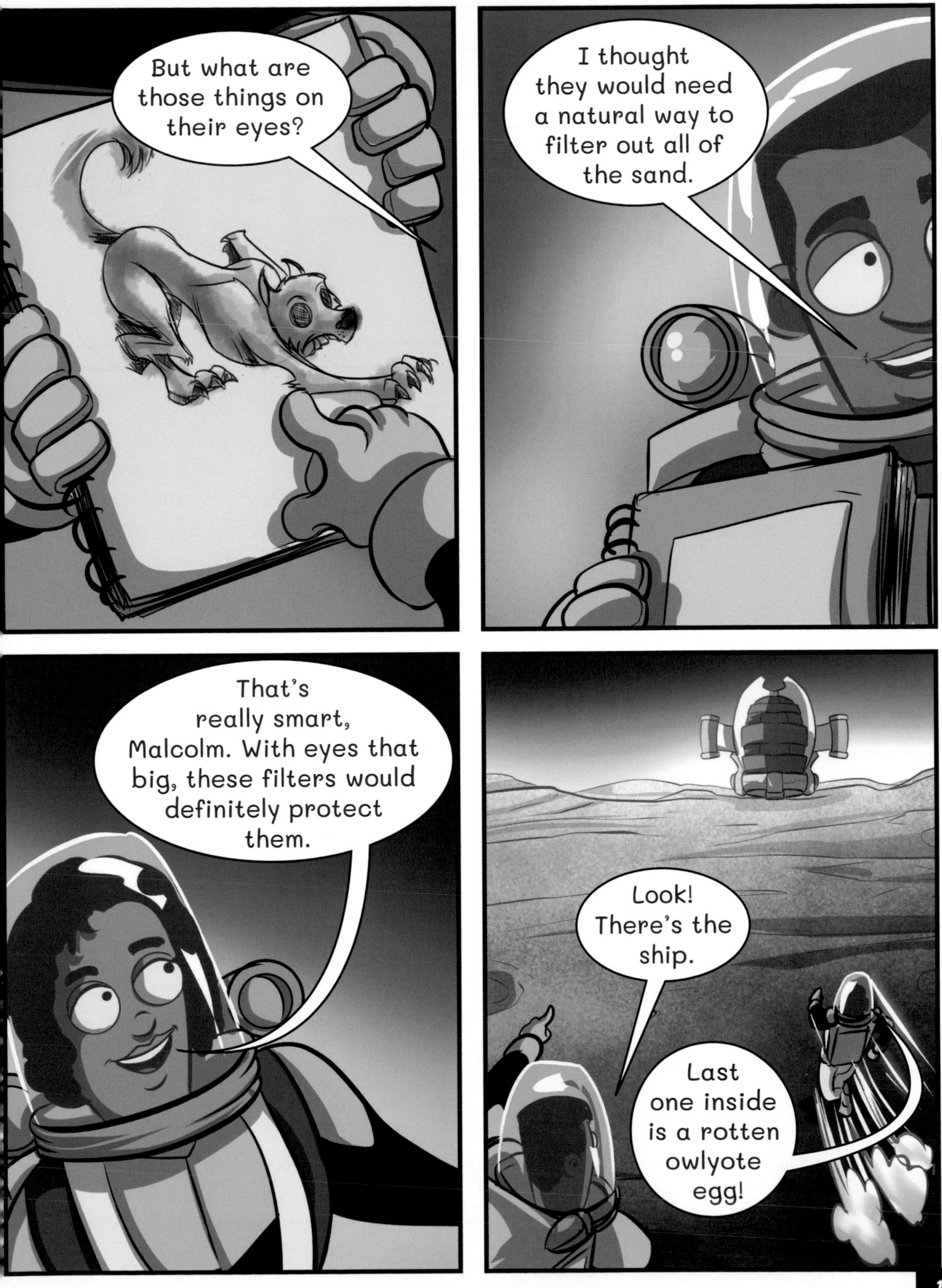
But what are those things on their eyes?
I thought they would need a natural way to filter out all of the sand.
That's really smart, Malcolm. With eyes that big, these filters would definitely protect them.
Look! There's the ship.
Last one inside is a rotten owlyote egg!

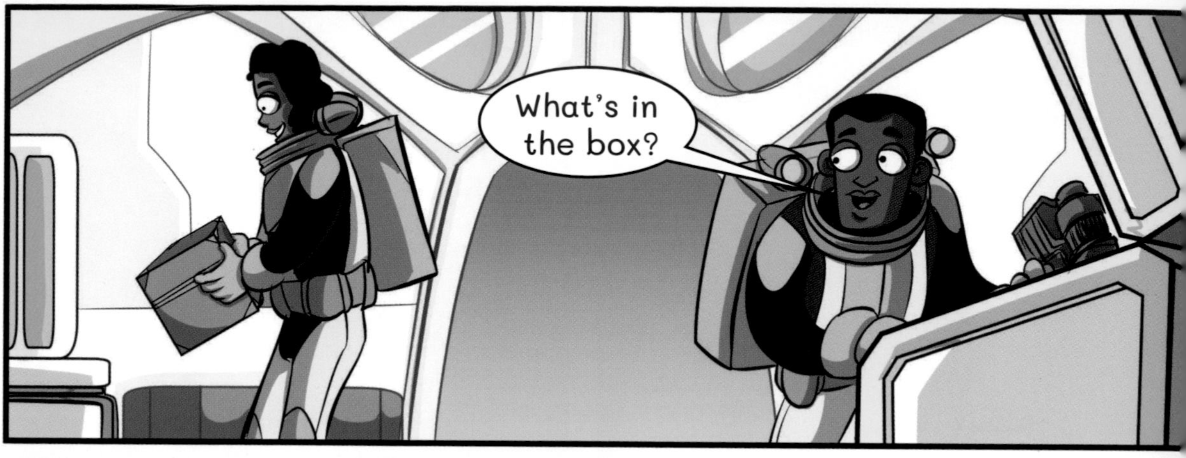
What's in the box?

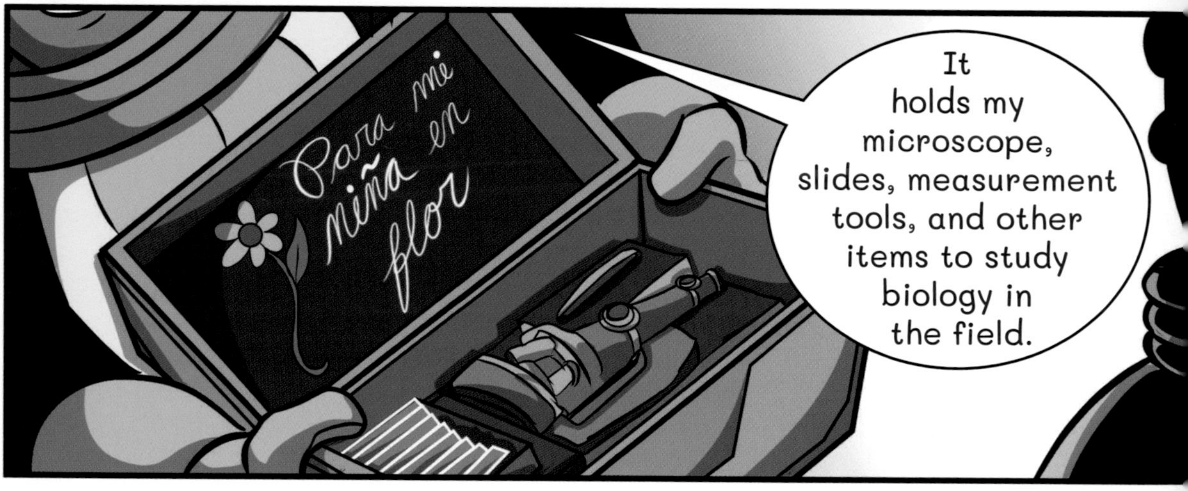
Para mi niña en flor
It holds my microscope, slides, measurement tools, and other items to study biology in the field.

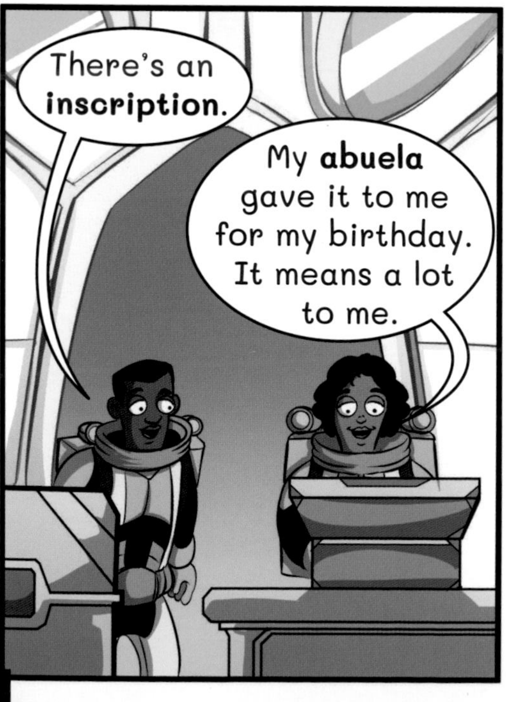
There's an **inscription**.
My **abuela** gave it to me for my birthday. It means a lot to me.

SCIENCE FACT

It is believed that scientists have identified only about 20 percent of the species living on Earth.

inscription: words carved into an object

abuela: grandma in Spanish

Dr. Thomas to kids. What is your status?

Hi, Dad.

We just finished your list.

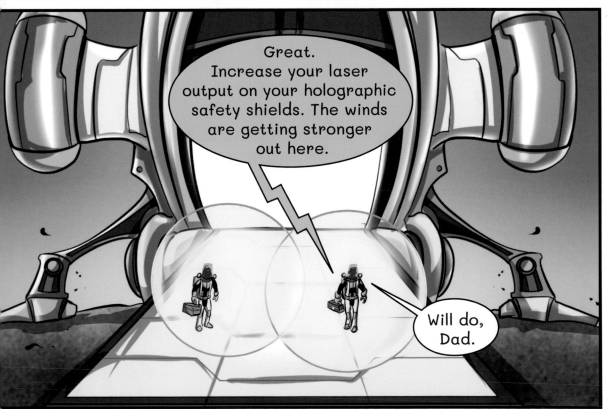

Great. Increase your laser output on your holographic safety shields. The winds are getting stronger out here.

Will do, Dad.

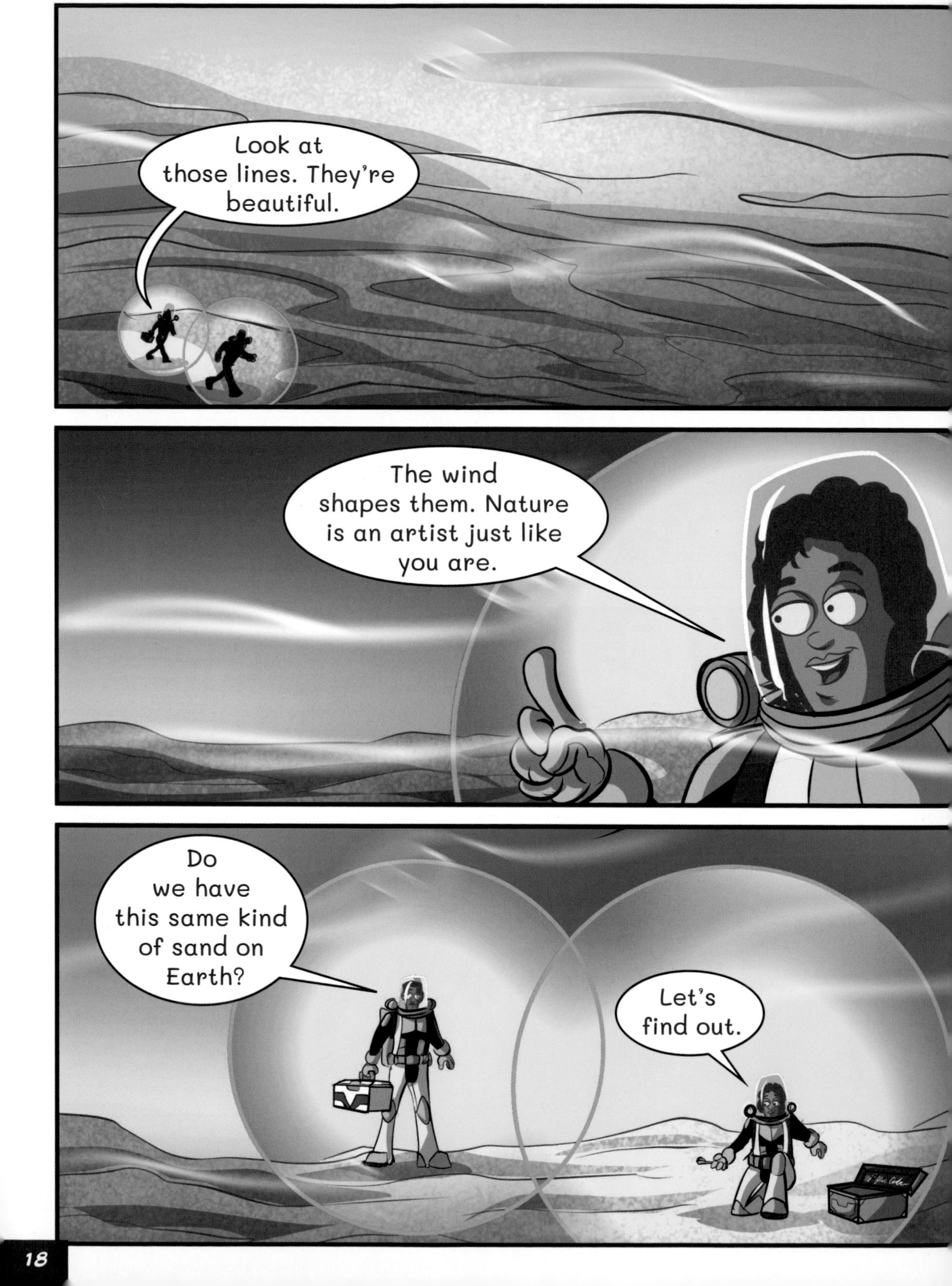
Look at those lines. They're beautiful.
The wind shapes them. Nature is an artist just like you are.
Do we have this same kind of sand on Earth?
Let's find out.

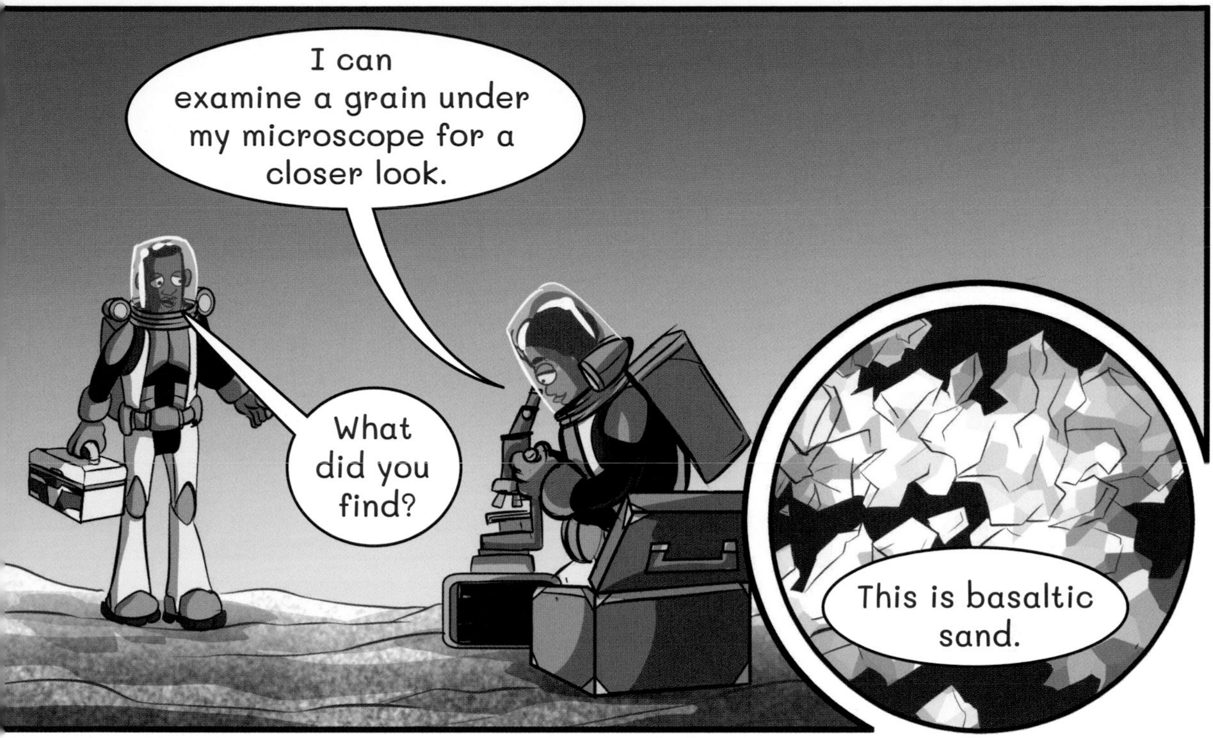
I can examine a grain under my microscope for a closer look.
What did you find?
This is basaltic sand.

SCIENCE FACT

Basaltic sand is made from basalt. Basalt is a volcanic rock that forms when lava comes into contact with water and cools quickly.

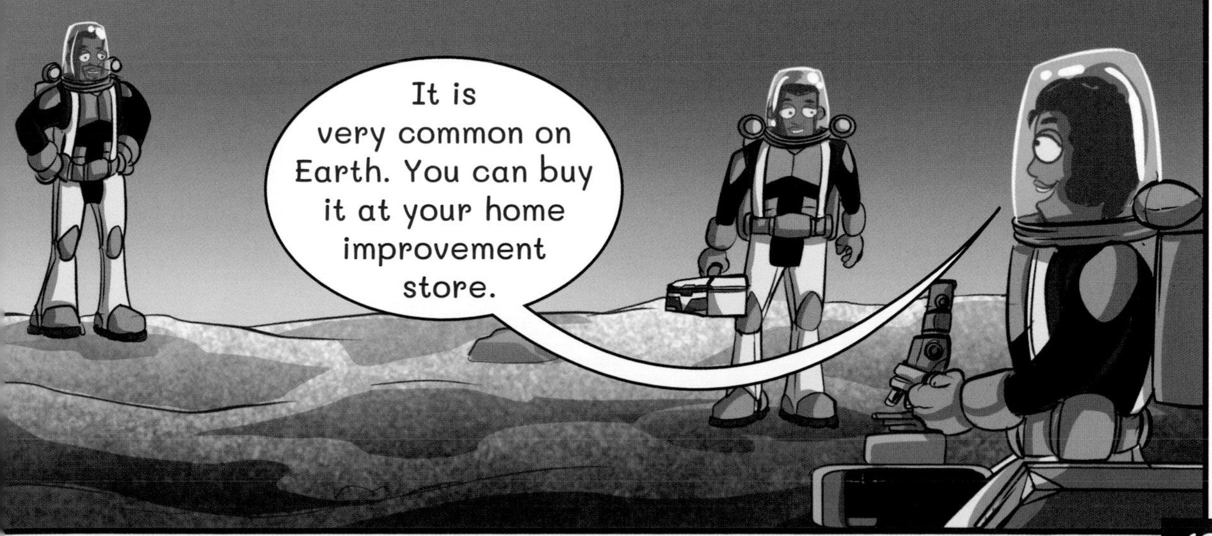
It is very common on Earth. You can buy it at your home improvement store.

Good work, kids. You found the parts and made a fascinating discovery.

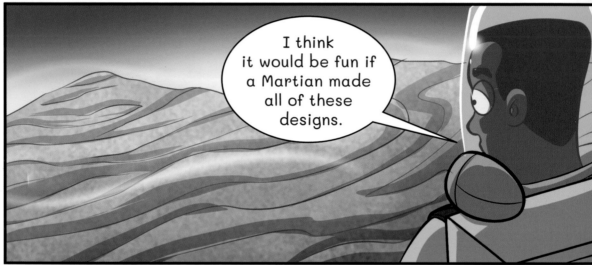

I think it would be fun if a Martian made all of these designs.

What are those things?

THE FUNDAMENTALS OF ART

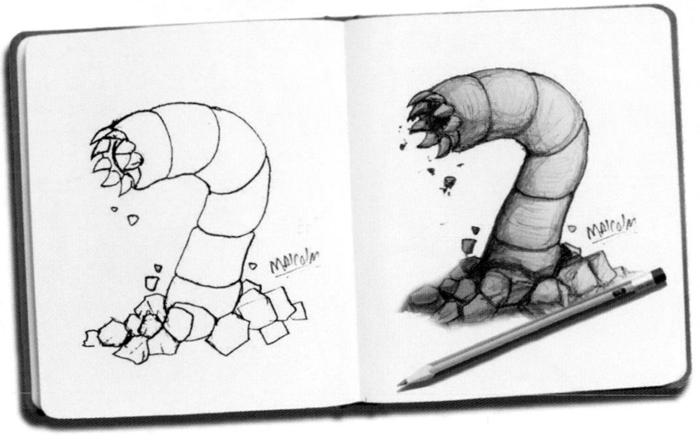
Malcolm
Malcolm

Let's put the FUN in the fundamentals of art by looking at the benefits of **shading** and how it can dramatically alter a drawing. Review these 2 images of Malcolm's sand weaver. Which looks more realistic?

•Shading a drawing like Malcolm did on the right gives an image depth and helps it appear more lifelike. Notice how instead of floating over the ground, the sand weaver now looks as if it is sitting on the surface of Mars.

•In art, an image without depth is called 2D (two-dimensional). That means the image is flat. It does not look like you could pick the image up or interact with it.

•An image with depth is called 3D (three-dimensional). That means the image looks as if it is existing in the real world. You could pick it up or interact with it.

•Next time you are drawing, try practicing shading to give your creations more life!

ARTIST TIP: Use your pencil like a crayon and fill in the area below what you have drawn to make it look like it is sitting on a surface.

shading: a technique used in drawing to show how light hits an object

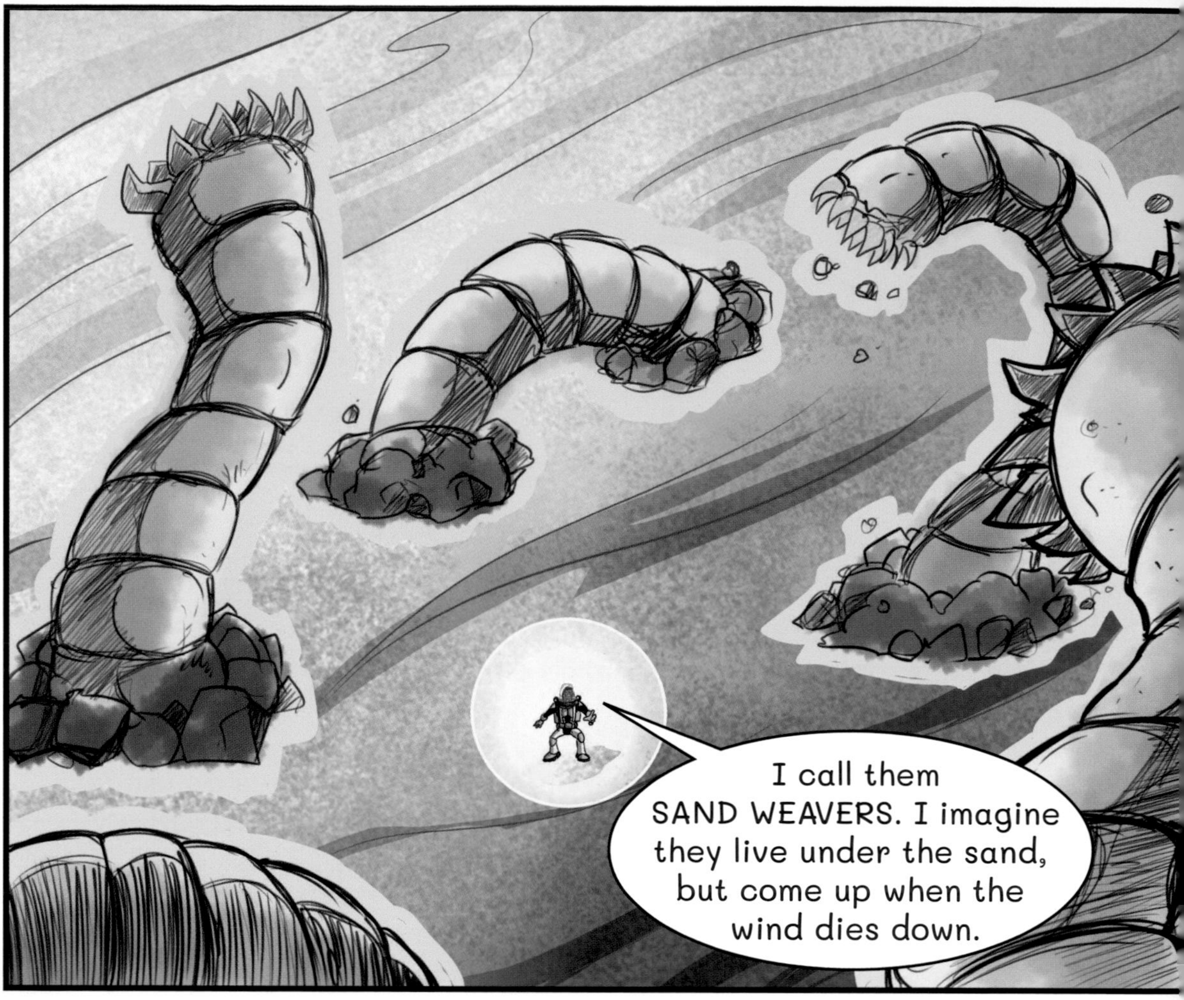
I call them SANDWEAVERS. I imagine they live under the sand, but come up when the wind dies down.

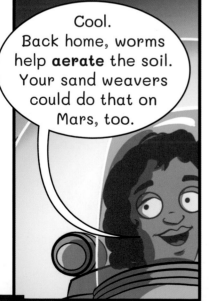

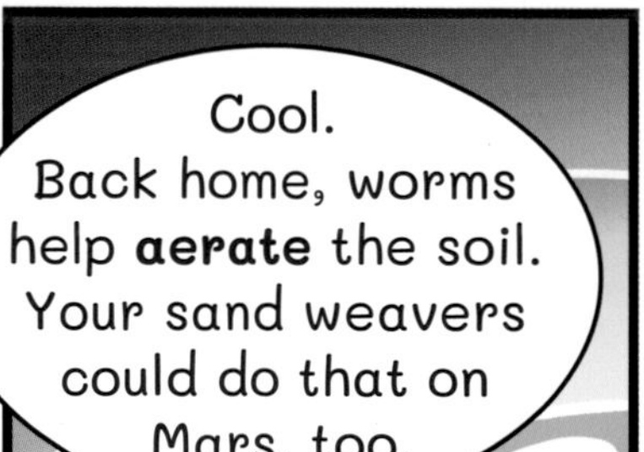
Cool. Back home, worms help **aerate** the soil. Your sand weavers could do that on Mars, too.

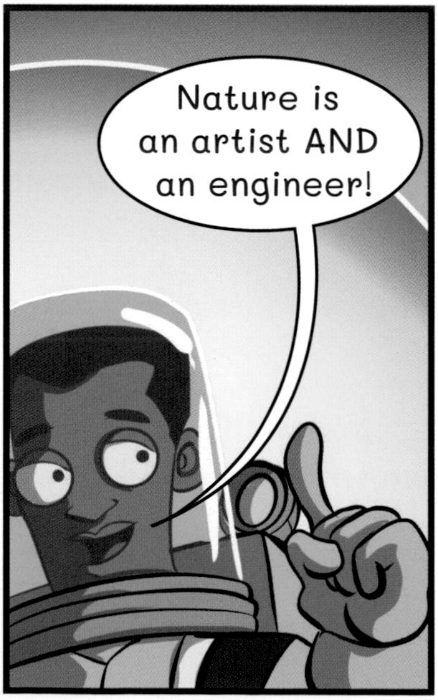
Nature is an artist AND an engineer!

SCIENC FACT

Earthworms help impr soil for plants. They a help aerate the soil w their burrows. That means water can trav down from the surfac more easily.

aerate: to fill somethir with air, like soil

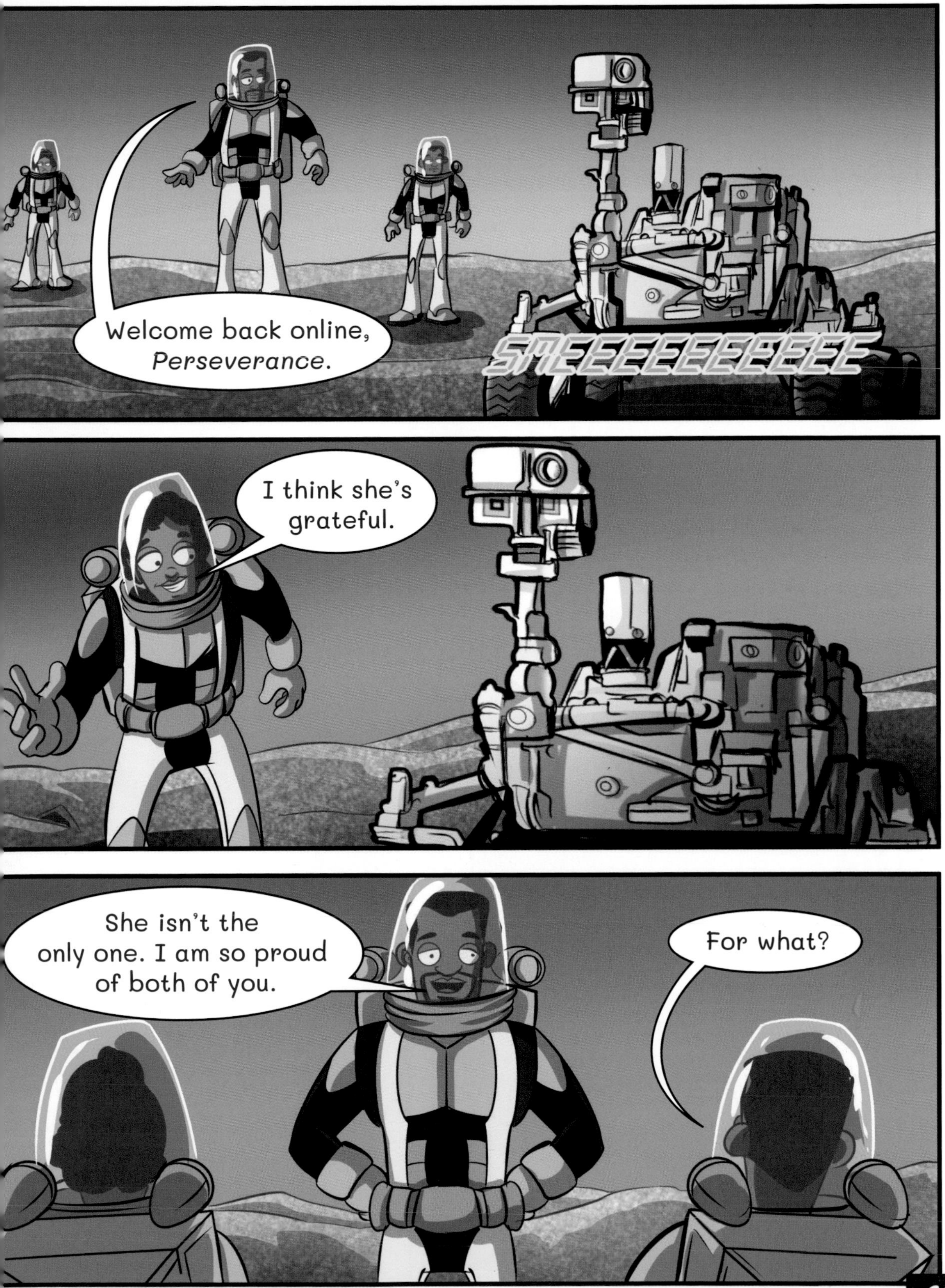
Welcome back online, *Perseverance*.
SMEEEEEEEEEEE
I think she's grateful.
She isn't the only one. I am so proud of both of you.
For what?

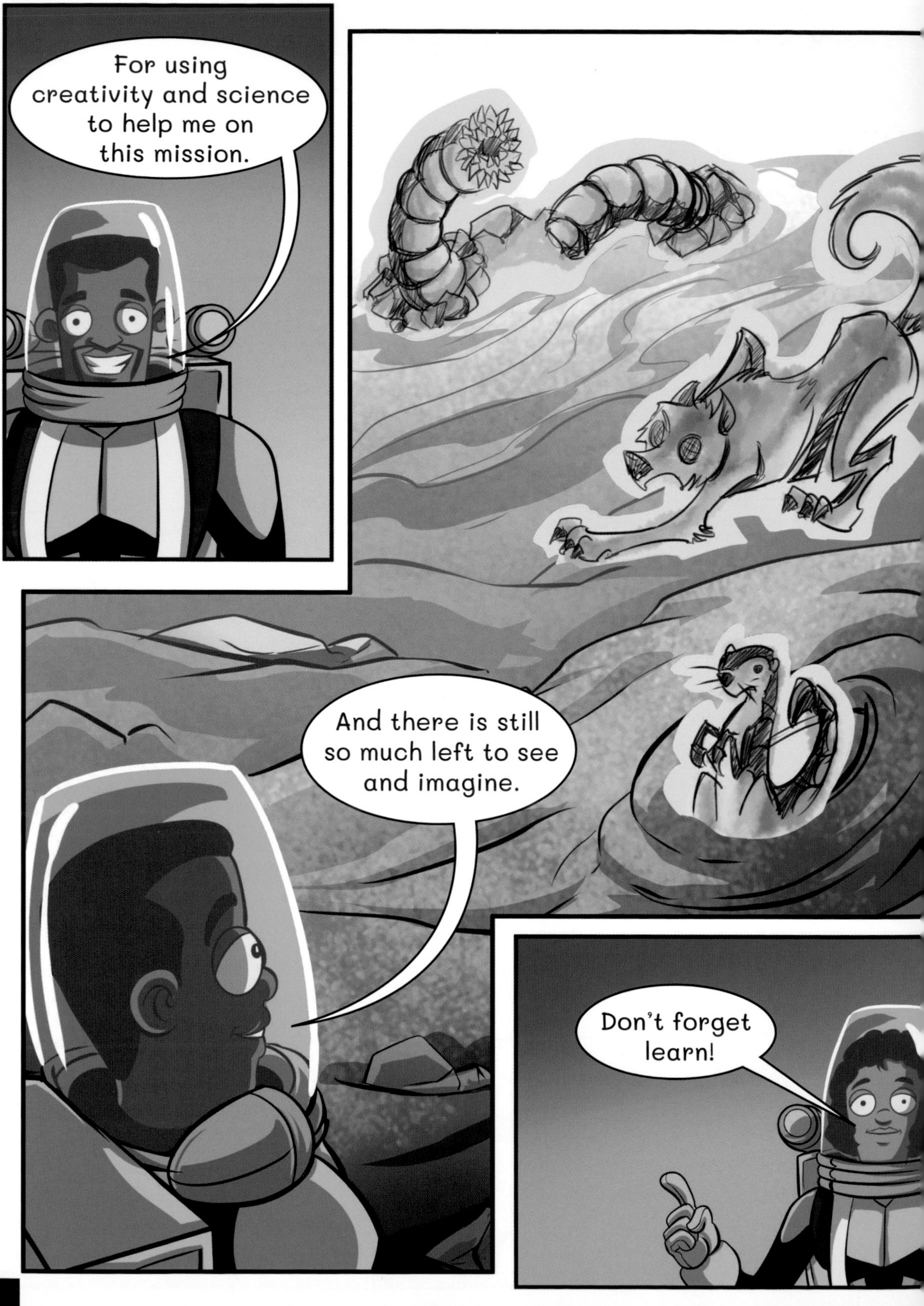
For using creativity and science to help me on this mission.
And there is still so much left to see and imagine.
Don't forget learn!

MARS SURVIVAL TIPS

Before making it off of Mars, you have to get there first. Here are some tips for making it to the Red Planet.

- You can't enter the shuttle without training. Typically, training for a mission into space takes an astronaut 18 months. (This is after 2 years of general training!)

- According to NASA, an astronaut needs 1,800 hours of training just to visit the space station.

- Astronauts need to have a wide range of knowledge and experience. They have to learn about everything from Earth sciences to engineering.

- Bring something to do. The trip to Mars will take 6 to 8 months, so be prepared to pass the time.

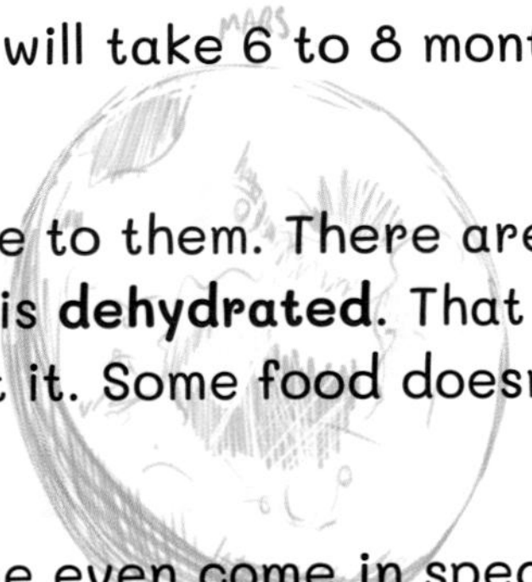

- Astronauts have a limited menu available to them. There are no refrigerators in space! A lot of the food is **dehydrated**. That means you just add water before you eat it. Some food doesn't need any prep, like fruit.

- All food is packaged here on Earth. Some even come in special packaging that keeps the food from floating away.

- Floating around all day is not easy! That's when your training comes in handy.

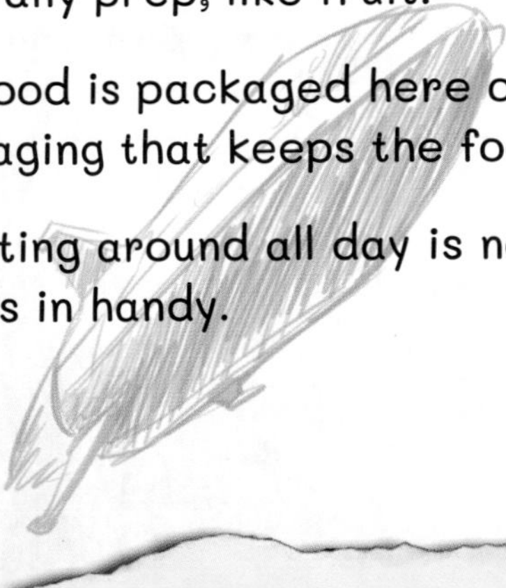

dehydrated: moisture removed from food to make it last longer

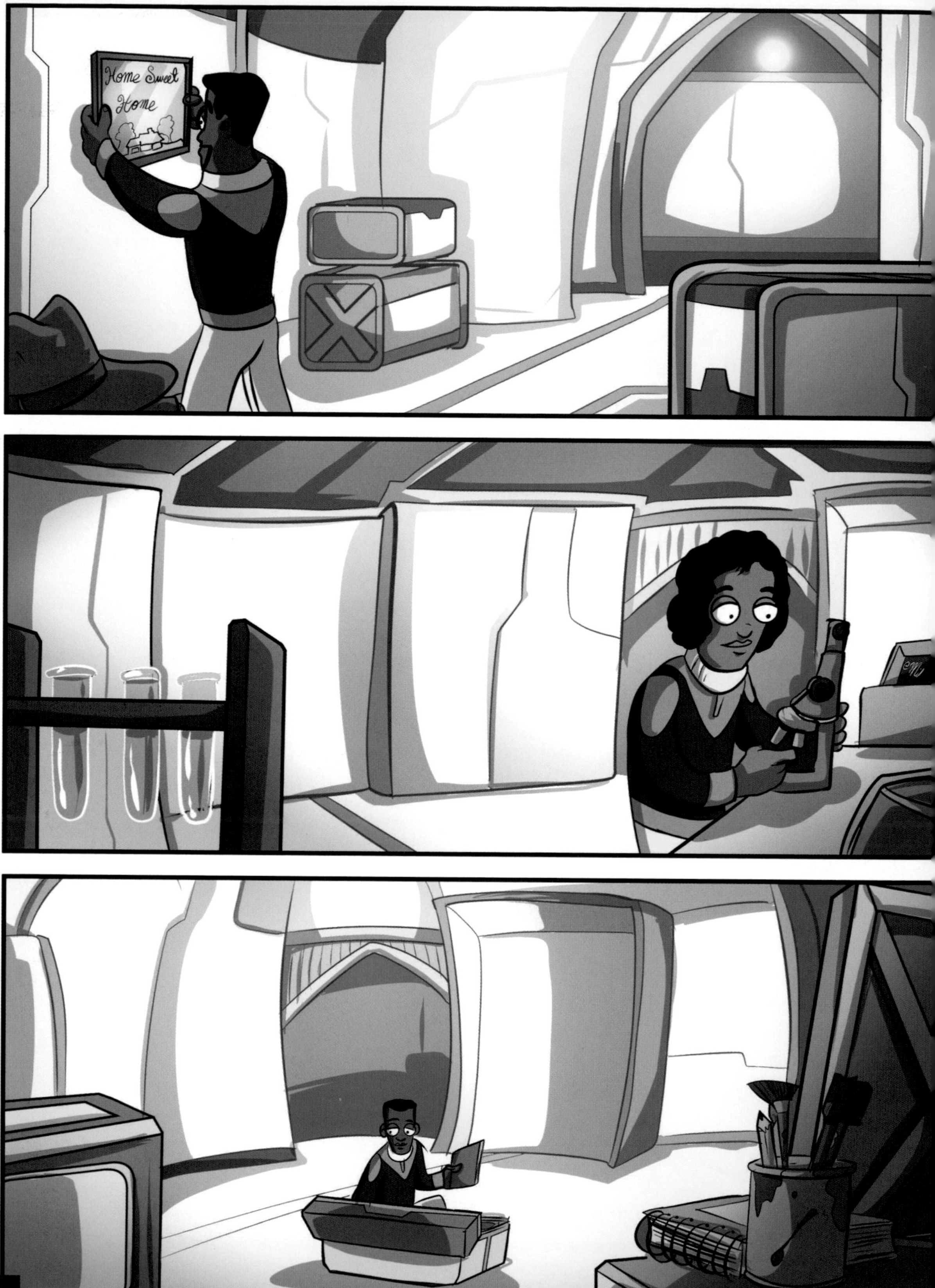
Home Sweet Home

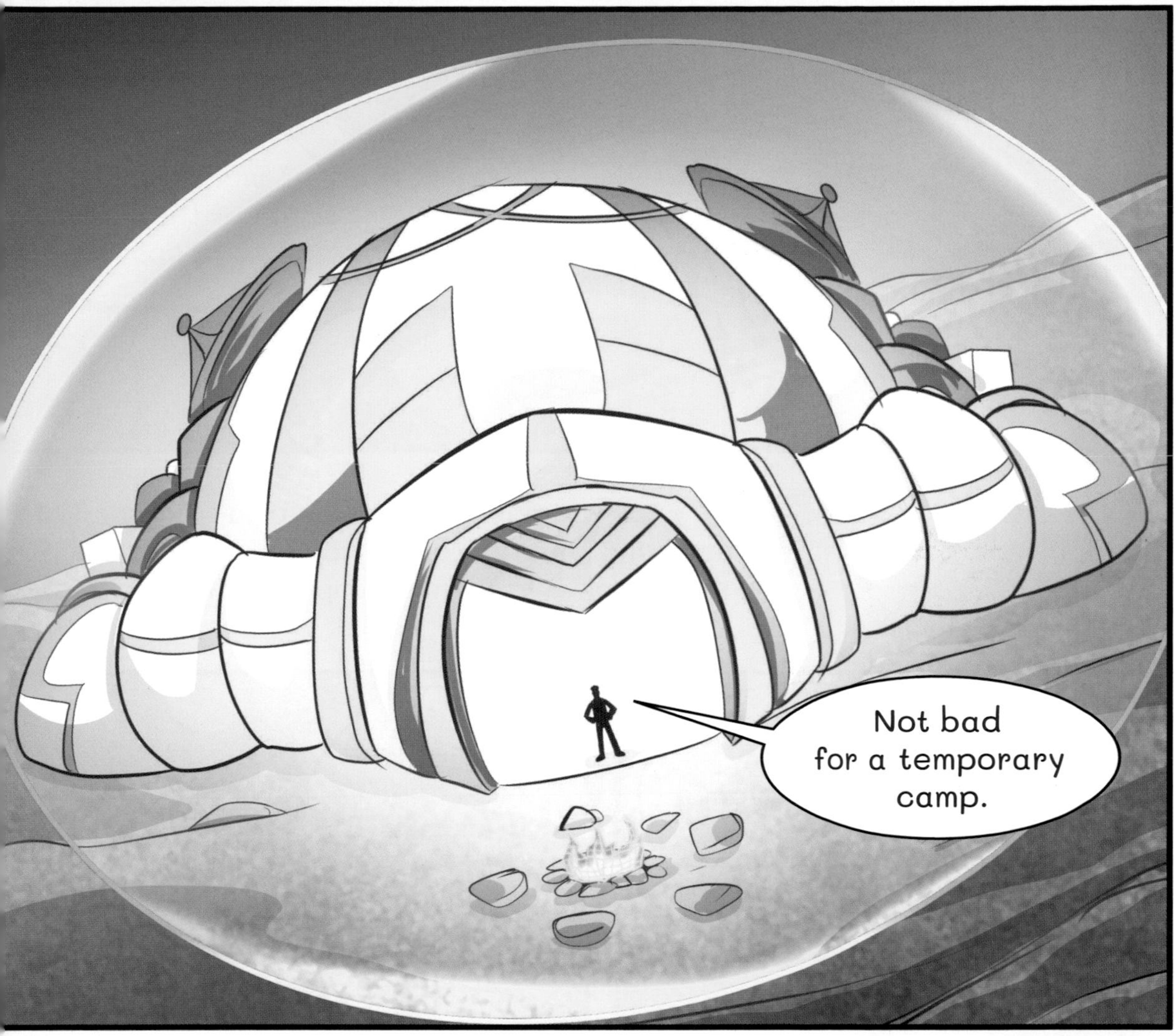
Not bad for a temporary camp.

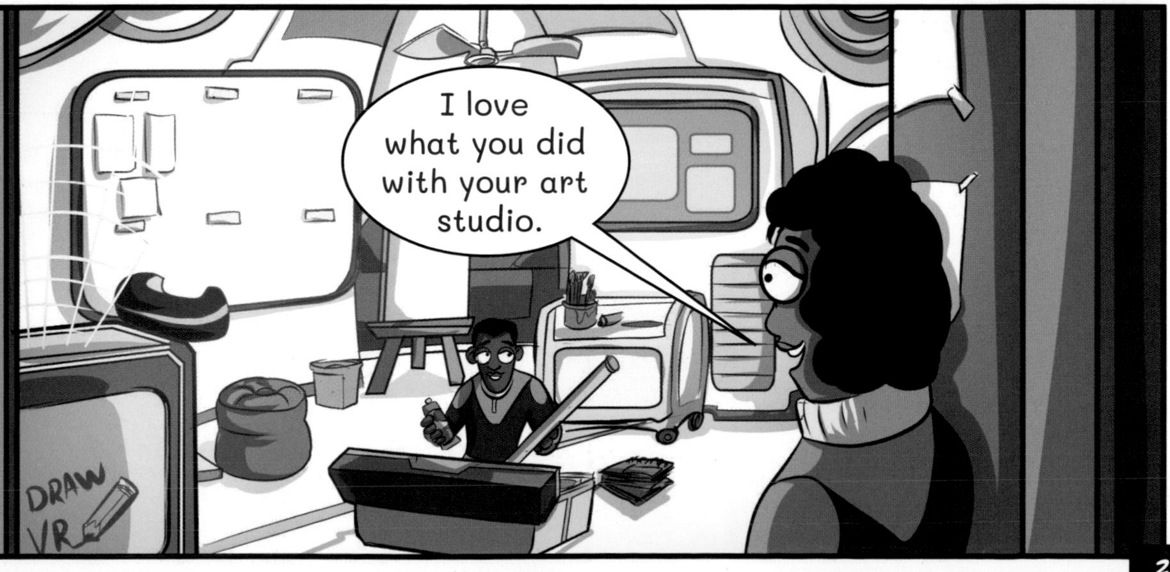
I love what you did with your art studio.
DRAW VR

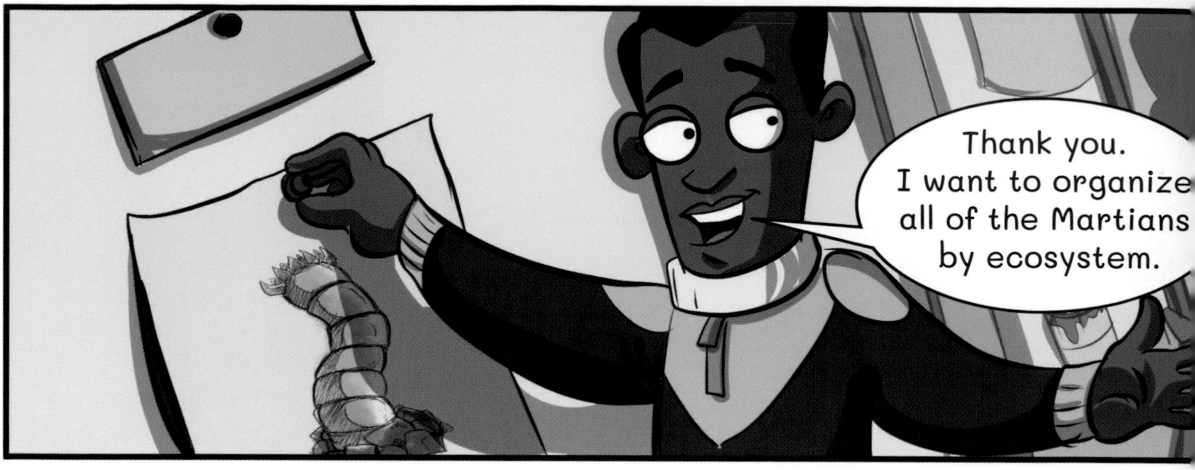
Thank you. I want to organize all of the Martians by ecosystem.

SCIENCE FACT

An ecosystem is a collection of all living and nonliving things in a particular place. Your backyard is an example of an ecosystem.

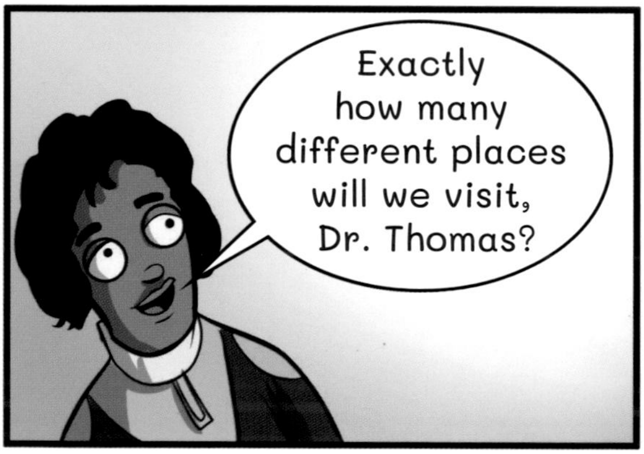
Exactly how many different places will we visit, Dr. Thomas?

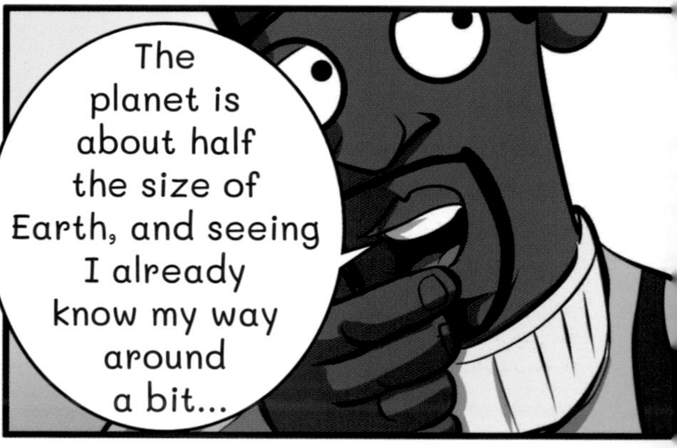
The planet is about half the size of Earth, and seeing I already know my way around a bit...

SCIENCE FACT

Fire requires oxygen and Mars does not have enough of this gas for a natural campfire.

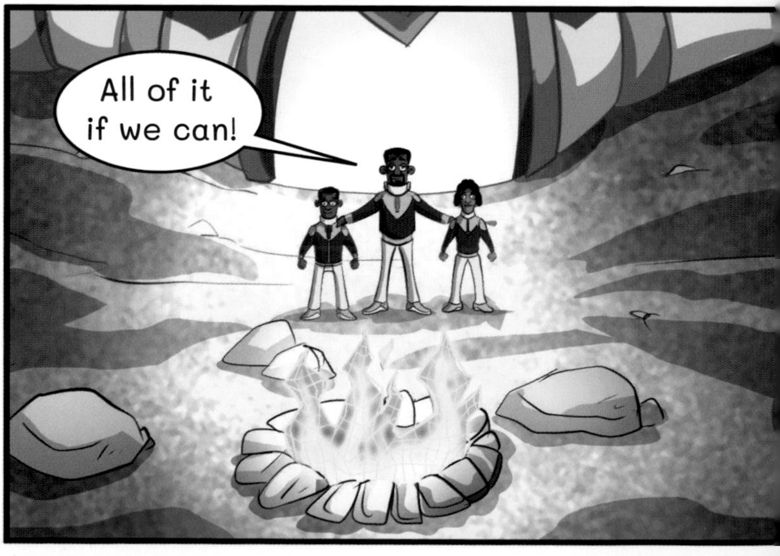
All of it if we can!

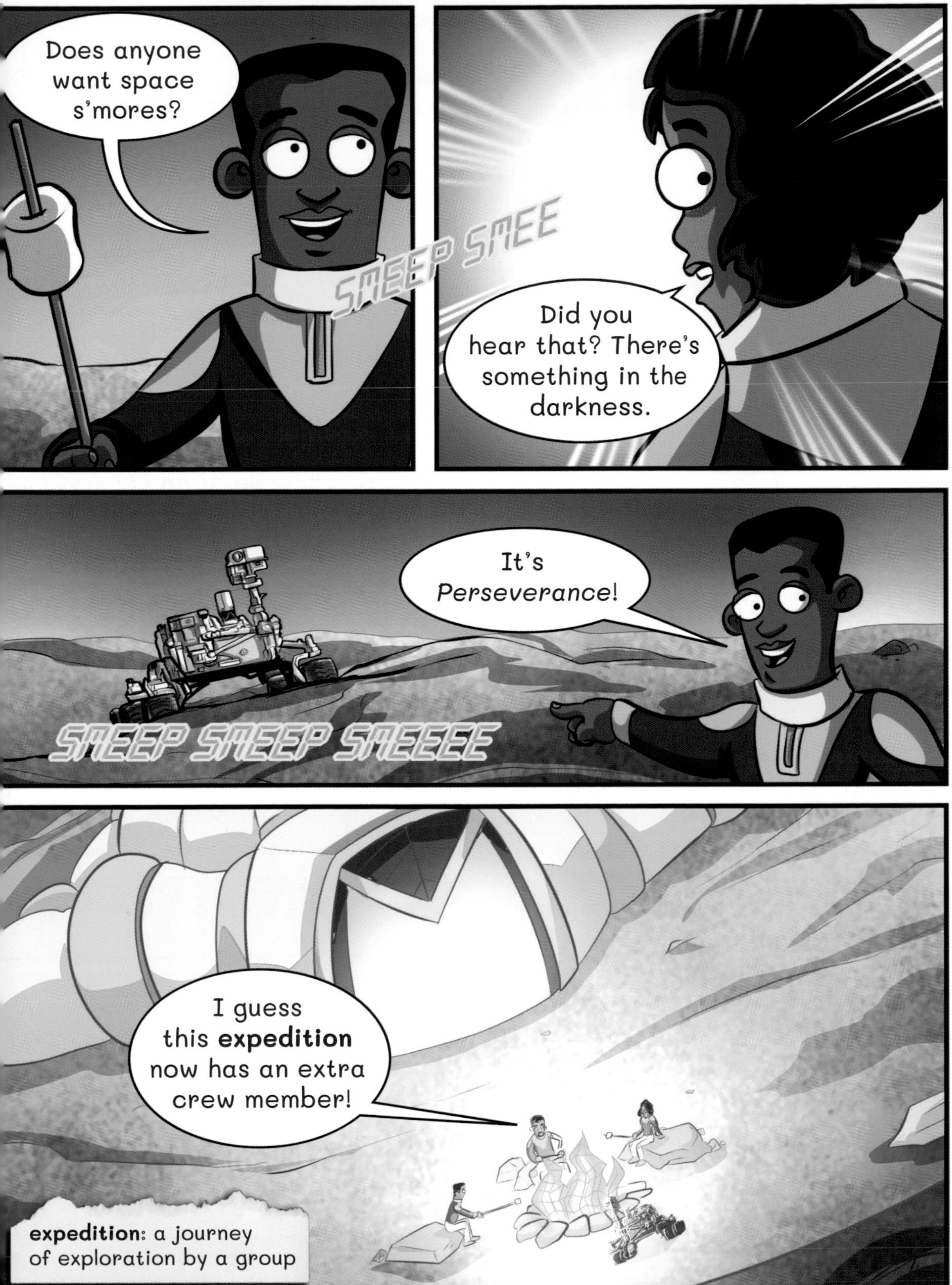

Does anyone want space s'mores?
SMEEP SMEE
Did you hear that? There's something in the darkness.
It's *Perseverance*!
SMEEP SMEEP SMEEEE
I guess this **expedition** now has an extra crew member!
expedition: a journey of exploration by a group

LASER FOCUSED

Malcolm and the crew used holograms on their Mars mission. But did you know that you can bring light to life right here on Earth with the help of an adult?

WHAT YOU NEED

- a piece of white paper
- glow-in-the-dark paint and paintbrush
- tape
- violet laser pointer

STEPS TO TAKE

1. Coat the piece of paper with glow-in-the-dark paint.

2. Tape the piece of paper to the wall in a dark room. Shut off the lights.

3. With the help of an adult, shine the violet laser pointer at the piece of paper. Streaks of light will appear on the page.

4. Use your creativity and make designs on the page or even draw a picture—WITH LIGHT!

SAFETY PAUSE

A laser pointer is not a toy. Use only under adult supervision and never shine directly into the eye.

LEARN MORE

BOOKS

Downs, Mike. *Imagining Space*. Vero Beach, FL: Roarke Educational Media, 2021.

Huddleston, Emma. *Explore the Planets*. Minneapolis, MN: ABDO Publishing, a division of ABDO, 2021.

WEBSITES

Curious Kids: Can People Colonize Mars?
https://theconversation.com/curious-kids-can-people-colonize-mars-122251

Kids ask, experts answer: Can we colonize Mars?

NASA: Perseverance
https://www.nasa.gov/perseverance

Learn about *Perseverance*'s mission to Mars and get all the latest news and discoveries.

THE MARTIANS

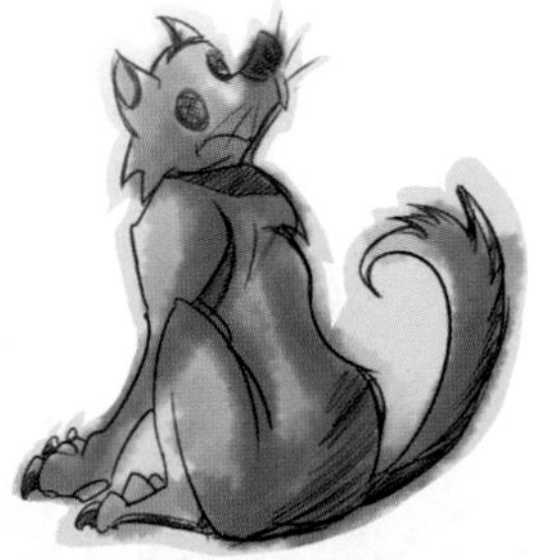

OWLYOTES

Malcolm draws these dog-sized, pack-dwelling Martians with thick, wire-like fur. They have filters on their eyes to protect them from the windswept sands of Mars.

SAND WEAVERS

Massive eyeless worms, Malcolm imagines that these Martians are behind the creation of the incredible designs that decorate the surface of the sand seas.

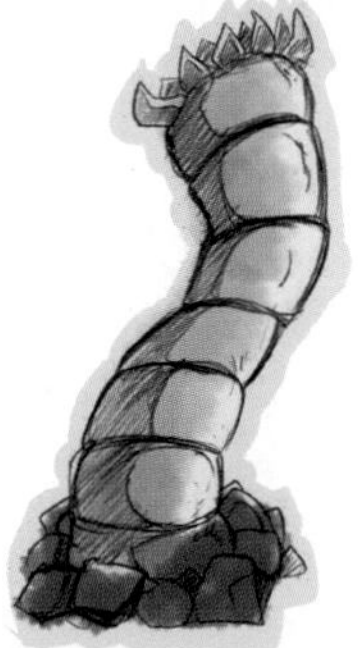

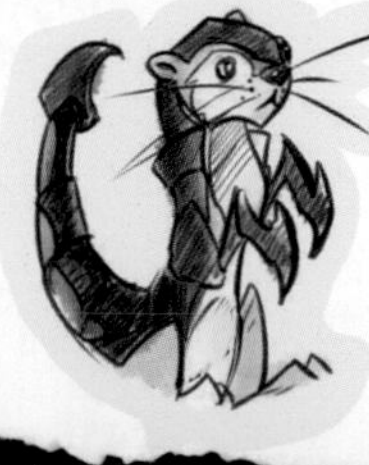

MEERSCORPIONS

Part lovable Meerkat and part alien arachnid, Malcolm imagines these Martians live in underground burrows throughout the sand seas of Mars.

GLOSSARY

abuela (uh-BWAY-luh) grandma in Spanish

aerate (EHR-ayt) to introduce air into something, like soil

atmosphere (AT-muhs-feer) a layer of gas that surrounds a planet

autonomous (uh-TAW-nuh-muhs) the ability to act on one's own without being controlled

dehydrated (dee-HY-dray-tud) moisture removed from food to make it last longer

distress (di-STRESS) something or someone is in danger

expedition (EK-spuh-di-shn) a journey of exploration by a group

exoskeleton (EKS-oh-ske-uh-tuhn) hard covering on some animals, like shells

holographic (hol-uh-GRAF-ik) created using laser lights

inscription (in-SKRIP-shuhn) words carved into an object

Martians (mahr-SHNZ) living creatures of Mars

native (nay-TIV) from a particular place

navigation (nah-vuh-GAY-shuhn) the process of accurately determining one' position, and then following a route

shading (SHAY-dingh) a technique used drawing to show how light hits an objec

terrain (te-RAIN) a particular geographic area

INDEX